DEATH DEFERRED

Warren Bull

Nine Bridges Press
Portland, Oregon

Also by Warren Bull

Novels
Abraham Lincoln for the Defense
Abraham Lincoln in Court and Campaign
Heartland

Short Story Collections
Manhattan Mysteries
No Happy Endings
Killer Eulogy and Other Stories

History
Abraham Lincoln: Seldom Told Stories

Cover art credits: Armand Garrido (mantis) and Antreina Stone (man); artist unknown (cityscape)

CHAPTER ONE

The words BREAKING NEWS crawled across the news ticker on the television monitor in the waiting room of the Campbell Hematologic Malignancies Clinic Infusion lab. This bold announcement was never the surprise news stations expected it to be, but then it was chased by the phrase: "Liam Conner named new ambassador to Razor Prime." My picture appeared on the screen. I went numb.

"Civil rights leader and head of the Freedom Party, Liam Conner, has been called by the interstellar Razor Collective to represent Earth on Razor Prime," said a woman.

My picture disappeared, replaced by a live shot of newscaster Janice Seymour. She was lovely in a professional kind of way. She had interviewed me in the past, and we were friends. I hoped her description of me would not get her in trouble. The Gunderson administration had long ago labeled me an agitator and leader of a group of lawless dissidents.

Seymour spoke to the camera: "We have not been able to locate Citizen Conner for comment. A spokesperson at Conner Construction told us he has taken a leave of absence from his business and is not expected to return in the near future. Conner has been chosen as so-called ambassador, which, of course, means he will be the next human sacrifice taken by our so-called intergalactic sponsors, the Razors. I'll be back with more about this breaking news story after this message."

I trembled. Sweat beaded on my forehead as I began to imagine my death. The pale man sitting opposite me five feet away tilted his bald head.

"I can tell them you're here," he said.

I took several breaths to pull myself out of the horror in my head. I stammered, "They'd probably pay you well for the information, but please don't," I said. "Imagine how pissed off President Gunderson will be when he finds out the Razors proclaimed a death sentence on a dying opponent."

"No worries," he said. "We who are about to die have to stick together. I'm Geoffrey Phelps. That was a good photo of you."

"Nice to meet you, Geoffrey," I said. We put our hands up, palms out, as if to give each other a high five, but we did not move closer together. "That photo was taken two years ago just after the regional senior division jujutsu finals."

"You won that event, didn't you?"

"Yes. The media like that photo. They never show the one taken after three Gunderson supporters ambushed me, clubbed me bloody, and the cops hauled me off to jail."

Seymour came back on the air and continued, "Because of the announcement of Conner's upcoming death, Action News wants to play a bootleg recording of part of his trial. You may remember Conner was accused of assaulting three alleged supporters of President Gunderson. The first person you will see on the tape is District Attorney Harvey Gray."

The video started. Gray, a heavyset man with white hair and a dark suit, stood a few feet from me where I sat on the witness stand in the courtroom. I recalled the stanky odor that hung like a cloud around him.

"Mr. Conner, how do you expect the court to believe you did so much damage to these men, when they had batons and you supposedly did not?" Gray asked, pointing to the table where the three thugs sat.

On the tape, I answered, "Well, Counselor, the batons are here as exhibits. The bullies are here, and, unlike the last time, they can't take me by surprise. If we push the tables back and give them their clubs, there should be enough room that I can show you how I did it right here and now."

The screen went black. Words showed on the screen: "Technical difficulties. We'll be right back. Please excuse the delay."

"Uh-oh," said Phelps. "Somebody didn't like that."

"Janice is a gutsy lady," I said.

"Do you think the One World Party had anything to do with you being chosen as the next Razor sacrifice?" asked Phelps.

"No. I don't think the party has any influence with the Razors. They see all humans as slugs they were forced to sponsor. I think they give as much thought to ambassadors as we give to the individual mosquitos we swat. It was just my bad luck. Like when my bone marrow started producing cancer cells."

My phone buzzed. I fished it out of my pocket and answered, putting the call on speaker. A robotic voice spoke: "You will appear at the launch pad in Cape Canaveral, Florida, by one AM local time tomorrow for transport to Razor Prime. Bring nothing with you, and be on time. We will be annoyed and you will regret annoying us if you fail to show up."

I couldn't be sure if the voice was a recording or a person, but I felt a need to respond.

"I am well aware of the carnage that followed the few ambassadors who tried to avoid going," I said. "I will not resist. However, as you can verify, I am currently in a medical facility in Portland, Oregon, awaiting treatment. The treatment is scheduled to take several hours, which will not leave enough time for me to make the rendezvous. I do not wish to cause you any inconvenience, such as providing individual transportation for me or delaying your schedule. Is there a later connection possible that would fit your requirements?"

A series of clicks followed.

"Your circumstances are confirmed. We rarely bother to visit your mudball of a planet. However, there is a trip scheduled by another species from your world to ours that would not inconvenience us unduly. Thirty days from now be at the ferry terminal in Anacortes, Washington, at one AM local time. Repeat the information."

"In thirty days at the ferry terminal, Anacortes, Washington. One AM."

The call disconnected.

Phelps was wide-eyed. "What are you going to do? No human ever survives face to face contact with the aliens."

"I have one month," I told him. "I'll tell the doctors to take the port out of my chest. Then I'll study everything written about these bastards, recover as much as I can physically, and live as long as I can before they kill me."

CHAPTER TWO

The world assumed I was already dead. I didn't contradict that idea. My impending death from cancer had already stripped my life of non-essentials. I gave final instructions about my will. I made final calls to the ones I loved. Then I isolated myself to review videos of first contact between our two species and pore over all other information I could find about the aliens. On one video, the Razor ship, flickering in and out of view, looked like a gigantic ant hill. It slammed into the ground in a clearing outside what looked like a scattering of primitive huts in the Guatemalan jungle. At the time, the area was actually a film set for a low-budget monster movie. The crew of Razors – with two arms, two legs, triangular heads, and antennae – resembled six-foot-tall, mottled green-and-brown praying mantises. The looked right at home on the set.

My stomach churned as I watched them butcher all the humans in the area by moving swiftly and using the razor-sharp outer edges of their forearms. They swarmed over the area, searching for others and slaughtering them, too, efficiently ensuring there would be no witnesses. One brave camerawoman recorded the attack on her cell phone. She surreptitiously dropped the phone and kicked it away before the aliens came for her.

Someone found the phone a couple of days later, when one of the film producers returned to the location from a meeting in Guatemala City and discovered the carnage. The images played to world-wide audiences. That prompted whatever extraterrestrial powers there are to insist that the Razors had to establish an ongoing relationship with the humans on Earth. The powers must have been major badasses because the Razors complied, despite their obvious loathing of our species and their resentment that they had to deal with us. There's a pecking order to everything, even intergalactic social orders, it seems.

I studied the few brief messages that had reached Earth from former ambassadors. They complained of being lost, hungry, and thirsty after landing on Razor Prime. Messages abruptly ended as a result of the death of an ambassador who interrupted an insectoid or didn't move out of its way quickly enough. Bothering a Razor was like getting between a mama grizzly and her cubs. I wondered if the powers that be here on Earth knew the fate of the ambassadors. Maybe they just didn't care.

My whole life I had been answering back to arrogant, annoying know-it-alls. Staying alive would be difficult.

...

On the specified date and time, I showed up in Anacortes and took a seat facing the main aisle. The terminal was so dimly lit that I didn't see anyone approach. I heard a squawk. Something poked my shoulder. A shadowy figure like a hump-backed gorilla grabbed my arm, twisted my hand so that it faced palm up and dropped a speck of something onto my hand. The dark creature mimicked putting something in its mouth.

I raised my other hand, which held a bottle of water, to get its attention. I gnashed my teeth, pretending to chew before swallowing. Next, I swallowed without chewing. No reaction. When I repeated the chewing motion, the figure slapped me hard across the face, bringing tears to my eyes, leaving my cheek red and sore. I felt the speck move on its own. I lifted my palm to my open mouth. Whatever was in my hand crawled into my mouth. I swallowed it, paused to calm my stomach, and then took a drink of water.

The being grunted. It took me a moment to decode its sounds. It was asking, "Followed you, who?"

6

"I don't know. I didn't see anyone."

The being disappeared. I stayed in the same spot, watching a series of words in red crawl again and again across a black chyron on the wall on the far side of the aisle. About five minutes later, the being reappeared.

"Who you told?"

"Nobody. I don't think anyone followed me tonight."

"Come."

I followed the shambling form.

Thank you for asking ... chewing, said a voice in my head. I did not want to die. Many have. Yes. Have many questions. Allow me time access memory. Slippery language. I will control it soon.

We walked up a rickety wooden gangway onto an old ferry. We crossed the deck. An oval hatch opened in a vessel I did not see clearly tied to the outer side of the ship. I paused, wondering if I would ever set foot on Earth again. I tried to burn in the scene, the constellations, the sound of water lapping against the pier, the smell of the harbor. The dark figure poked me in the back. I sighed and stepped through into an aqua mist.

...

I awoke cold and shivering. My head reeled. My stomach hurt. I opened my eyes a crack. I was stretched out naked on a pallet in an ashy gray space smaller than a prison cell. The cells I have been in after protests looked and smelled better than this.

The voice in my head spoke. *If you need to ...up throw? Throw up? The raised oval in the corner is the proper location for waste.* Rancid odors emanated from that direction.

"Is there something I can put on?" I asked. "I'm freezing."

There are bed coverings and clothing in a drawer under your bed.

I pulled on a robe so scratchy against my skin that it might have been made from gunny sacks.

"So, voice in my head, who and what are you? What can I call you? Do I need to speak or can you read my thoughts?"

I am a biological universal translator in terms of function. I can understand if you think about me or talk to me. Most of your thoughts are clear, although I don't understand all of the references and images yet. It paused. As to what to call me, you cannot pronounce the designation my species would use for me. Perhaps you should choose a name.

I thought for a moment. "There is a famous fictional character that advised another fictional character who, like me, had no idea what the existence he was thrust into was like. I think I'll call you Jiminy Cricket. Jimmy for short. So how long will you be with me, Jimmy?"

Jimmy. I like that. I will be with you for the rest of your life, which, of course, will not be for long.

"And after that?"

No one knows. I try not to get too attached to this life since it will end shortly.

"Do you like being alive?"

Well, I suppose I do.

"Perhaps with your help, we can extend both of our lives for a bit. In simple terms, what can I expect on the ship and on Razor Prime?"

I do not understand a great deal. But the ship and the world depend on the equivalent of money. As an ambassador, you are entitled to transportation to the planet, food, board, and clothing. At the expense of your hosts, of course. You draw a daily, um, wage starting from when you were named to your post.

"So, I have some credits already," I said.

Yes, but I would be cautious about spending them for better quarters or food. You will need them later to have any chance of extending our existence. If you accept the current circumstances, you will accumulate a few more before we arrive. Any service you provide will be compensated, based on the value of the service. That is a matter of honor. Honor is greatly valued and protected. Insults are punished severely. Anything might be considered a slight by an insectoid in a bad mood. And they're always in a bad mood. Any being not descended from an insectoid is considered a lesser being and subject to the whims of the insectoids. Any ordinary insect likewise exists only to serve the royal Razor family. As insectoids, they can have as many as twenty eggs in one egg sack. When hatched, the nymphs look like fully developed small adults. They don't require intense and sustained care like human newborns do, so killing an individual has little emotional significance for adult Razors.

I knew people like that on Earth. At that moment, I heard a voice from outside my head. It sounded like it came over a cheap radio.

"Conner, this is the Captain of the vessel. Are you listening?"

"Yes, uh, sir, I am," I answered.

"We are on the way to your destination. By custom, no one of us will have direct contact with you. Better accommodations are available at your request. We will provide nutrition at the next scheduled mealtime, which, unfortunately, is some hours away. We can bring you something sooner and tastier if you like. There would, of course, be a small charge for those amenities."

"That is kind. Thank you, Captain, but the scheduled meal and the current room are sufficient for my needs."

"The Razors ask if you have any information that might be of interest to them," said the captain. "My advice would be not to waste their time with complaints."

"Thank you again, Captain. I think they might be interested in how someone found out about the pick-up location. It had to be at the time I repeated the instructions over my phone. It might have come from the patient I was talking to, but more likely my phone was being monitored by someone in the Gunderson administration. They must have had me under surveillance. They probably bugged my phone."

"I will pass that along. Is there anything else?"

"Yes, sir. If there is some simple task that I can perform for you and your crew on the voyage, I would be happy to be of whatever small assistance I might be."

"It's not likely, but I will consider it."

Well done.

The Captain spoke up again immediately.

"Good news, Conner. The Razors found your information to be of interest. That very rarely happens. They paid for the favor. You can easily afford better quarters than those you occupy now."

"Whoa, Captain, that was a quick answer. No time lag at all.

Thank you kindly, sir, but where I am is entirely adequate. Much as I value your offer, my finances are unlikely to improve so…."

The Captain cleared his throat. "Razors are efficient. They listened, decided, and disconnected in seconds. It is not good business for me to disappoint them. You will be moved to a more comfortable location at no cost to you. And there is an opportunity for more fiscal gain that we can discuss later."

CHAPTER THREE

Aware that I was oddly warm and comfortable, I did not want to open my eyes. I was tempted to drift back to sleep, but that would not help me prepare for my life on Razor Prime. Opening one eye, I looked around. The walls were beige. There was no window. I opened my other eye. Over me was an authentic handsewn quilt; beneath me, a genuine bed, with a real mattress. Nearby, a white terrycloth robe hung from a nearby hook.

Conner, I have questions about your body.

"Okay," I said.

Unhealthy cells in your blood are reproducing too quickly and invading your bone marrow.

"Yes, they are."

If I'm not mistaken, you took poison to kill them, which also killed other fast-growing cells.

"I did in the past, but no longer."

Why would your body create things that endanger your health? I don't understand. Is it preparation for a change?

"It is an error," I explained. "A genetic mutation. It pushes for a change from living to dead. I poisoned myself and took other drastic measures to try to stop the process. For some time, I was able to keep it at bay, but it is winning the struggle."

This is not a good thing.

"Absolutely correct."

I have informed the Captain.

11

"I didn't know you could do that."

I can communicate with others. It is somewhat unorthodox to speak to anyone except you, but I thought he should be aware. He is obligated to deliver his cargo intact. The consequences for offloading damaged goods are severe.

"Okay, Jimmy. What should I do now?"

Eat.

Bowls of stuff resembling weeds sat on a table in my new spacious cabin. When I started eating, I discovered I was ravenous.

"Comfortable, Conner?" came the voice of the Captain.

"It's very nice, sir," I answered.

"Conner, there is no reason for you to mention my little joke about asking you for a surcharge."

"Of course not, sir. There's nothing wrong with asking."

"Speaking of which, I do have a small task you'd be able to do. It is not in the least bit dangerous, but it is somewhat unpleasant. I'd be willing to employ you at the standard rate for a planetsider."

"Planetsider?" I asked, curious about that word. I wondered if it was used like the term *landlubber* among sailors.

The Captain chuckled. "You don't negotiate like a planetsider. As you say, there is no harm in asking. Very well, I'll pay you as an ordinary crew member. That's the best I can do."

"And the duties, Captain?"

"We're hauling a Plix ambassador's third-level assistant and her belongings to the Razors. Her name is Ky. She is constantly complaining. Ky bangs on the wall and screams when ignored. She demanded to speak to Someone of Importance and I immediately thought of you."

It was my turn to laugh. "So, what are the Plix like, besides obnoxious?"

"They look quite a bit like Razors and the two can breed together. Like the Razors, they are obsessed with status. Maybe that's because both races are so insignificant in the universe. The third level dumps on the fourth through tenth levels. They are despised by the second and first levels. Any perceived slight can result in a duel to the death. You used to be able to tell commoners from the elite because the elite were larger, but that's not so anymore. Of course, mammals like us, as well as avians and other species are beneath notice and can be squashed for any reason. This one is especially prickly. She's upset that her government booked her on a working freighter instead of a luxury liner. We usually haul bodies from Razor Prime to Plix Prime. So, her booking was an intentional insult. If the embassy doesn't send a special limo to pick her up, we'll probably carry her carcass or the body of whoever she challenges on our return trip. I doubt if you can stop her complaints, but, if I can avoid it, I'd rather not have another negative report on the record."

"If you allow me to cut her off when I say the word 'final,' I'll take the job," I said.

...

"You have to rescue me," demanded Ky as I entered her room.

"Who the hell are you?" I shot back.

In a tone of voice I usually associate with rat terriers, she gave me a lengthy answer ending with third-level assistant.

"Third-level assistant? Is this a joke? When I find out who put through a third-level, somebody will pay for this outrage. One of my staff will get back to you, Ky. Eventually."

"Wait, sir," she pleaded. "Please. Since you are talking to me already, give me a chance to explain."

"I bet it was that damn Captain who connected you to me. He didn't like it when the Razors insisted he give me better lodgings without paying him more. It's against my better judgment to waste my time with you. Just get to it. I have better things to do."

She railed on for five minutes. I wondered how she managed to breathe without stopping her yapping.

"Enough," I cut in. "Even a mere third level should not have to put up with such disrespect. I shall speak about this myself. You will not bother me or anyone on the ship again. It would undercut my intervention on your behalf. I've listened. Now I will take the appropriate action. That is more than sufficient. I will not speak with you again. That is final."

It felt good to treat her like she treated others. Who knew when I would be able to safely put a snob in their place again?

CHAPTER FOUR

There was no way to track how long the flight took, let alone how many days or weeks had passed on Earth. I spent time exercising, eating, sleeping, and wondering what was going to happen when I arrived. I pressed Jimmy for anything else he knew that he could tell me about Razors and Plix.

As I said before, Razors and Plix are infamous for their short tempers and violent outbursts. Nowadays, breeding females in elite families receive a special diet and medical attention to ensure healthy, intelligent offspring. Prospective mothers are strictly monitored and allowed to get pregnant only at specified times. Only one in ten nymphs join the elite family. The others are fostered by ordinary families who favor them over the progeny of their own because they are more likely to improve the family fortune. Nymphs with two commoner parents are still theoretically considered a possible food source during a famine.

I nodded before I spoke: "I've been fighting against that kind of thinking all my life, Jimmy. My family is as distinguished as a single grain of sand on a beach. In about 1800 an author named Jonathan Swift suggested something like that in an essay titled 'A Modest Proposal.' I don't remember the details, but I read it and enjoyed it."

It will still be in your memory. I'll search for it and read it when I have time. Don't worry; my puttering around in your memory won't disturb you. I can do it while you sleep and stay alert when you're awake.

14

At one time I would have worried that Jimmy would find out my moments of cowardice and cruelty. I was no saint. But concern about what others thought about me was one of the things that my approaching death had persuaded me to relinquish. I snorted at the thought.

"Well, I hope I've led a sufficiently interesting life that you won't get too bored. I regret not doing things I could have done more than I regret anything I have done. Regarding the insects, I guess nobody has figured out that fostering will eventually mean that the elite and the ordinary will have much of the same genetic heritage," I said. "Come to think of it, commoners would have greater genetic variability because of a bigger gene pool. That would give them a biological advantage in resistance to diseases and fewer inherited disorders. Maybe they have it already."

At this moment we were both engaged in sycophancy, which was far from my usual attitude. My habit of talking back to bullies got me beaten up by other kids until I started martial arts training. I started with wrestling and then moved on to jujutsu training. On the new planet, any step away from total spinelessness might well be immediately fatal. I was not used to cowering before anyone.

I shared what is common knowledge in the universe. My species shares information with each other and we gather knowledge for future generations, but none of us assigned to human ambassadors has lived long enough to learn much of anything beyond the landing bay. Young Razors prowl the docks looking for aliens they can kill.

I had long practiced jujutsu, with special attention to speed and agility. I also worked on kicking techniques that a friend of mine, a Taekwondo teacher, had shown me. Maybe it wouldn't spare my life, but at least I might have a nasty surprise for an attacker.

"Conner," announced the Captain. "We will arrive soon. Surprisingly, I enjoyed having you as a passenger. I usually dump humans off first so the young Razors hoodlums can kill them quickly. That way they don't interfere with the rest of the unloading. I'm going to leave you for last. The local riffraff will get bored and go off to kill somewhere else by then. I'll leave your wages and the key to the Earth embassy outside your door."

"Thank you, Captain. I have a request. I hope I have the funds to pay you for it."

When I explained, the Captain laughed and promised to help me for free. My wages took the form of a pot-metal teardrop-shaped pendant with a piece of gravel mounted in the center. It came on a pendant on a thin gray metallic chain. Jimmy advised me to wear it next to my skin under the work shirt and overalls the Captain provided. An odd multipronged ceramic and metal doodad also hung from the chain. Completing my outfit were grimy work boots with steel toes and steel shanks that, luckily enough, actually fit me and a dirty red bandana that I wrapped around my head. I left by a service door, carrying one piece from a massive pile of Ky's luggage down to the dock.

An assortment of beings resembling earth insects, sea creatures, and birds looked me over when I joined the line unloading the vessel, but maybe because I was helping, they said nothing. Their clothing varied by body type, but they covered their bodies with the equivalent of one or two-piece earthly work clothes. I said nothing but took my turn going up empty-handed and returning down the gangplank with her paraphernalia, which we stacked on the ground while we waited for something in which to load it.

Activity on the dock continued at a steady pace for about fifteen minutes. Box after box formed a mound that would have filled a cargo van back on Earth. Eventually, a sturdy hovercraft with peeling paint floated around a corner and settled to the ground near the heap. The open bed of the craft was half-filled with cargo.

A voice I recognized barked out from the hovercraft, "Hurry up. I have to get to the Capital. What is taking you dung beetles so long? Driver, help them with my things."

The transport driver, who sauntered over, looked humanoid. On a dark night in a thick fog he might have passed for human. From his casual clothing, it was evident that this guy was a trucker, not a chauffeur. The Plix remained out of sight inside the vehicle, no doubt seething about being treated like baggage and plotting revenge for what she saw as a mortal insult. After a moment she screeched, "Be careful. Those are worth more than all of your flea-bitten hides put together."

"Bitch," the driver muttered. "I'd love to break a few of her pre-

16

cious things, but they would literally kill me if I did."

I sidled up to him. "What if she arrives late?"

"Great loss of face. Humiliation."

I nodded. "Who owns the other cargo?"

"More important people. The cushioned items lashed down in the middle belong to the Plix ambassador. They're fragile and extremely valuable."

"Hey, where do you want your junk?" I yelled out to Ky.

"It's not junk, you idiot," she snarled. "Move it carefully. One scratch and I'll hang your stuffed head on the wall. I want my possessions tied down firmly in the middle."

"Is that an order, ma'am?" asked the driver.

"Yes. Wait." She was silent for a moment. "There. I've entered it into the record with my official mark. No more questions. Disobey me at your peril."

The workers stood around, showing no interest in loading. I waved at the worker who had carried the heaviest loads by himself and pointed to the cushioned items. He put his fingers on a crushingly heavy crate. I motioned to two other workers.

"Careful, you. You heard the lady," I said to the others.

The three workers got in each other's way as they groaned and shuffled theatrically along with the load that one had previously managed with no trouble by himself. The driver unobtrusively directed the heaviest items placed on the most delicate. After the load was in, the dockworkers made four attempts before successfully tying everything in place. A creature looking somewhat like an over-grown possum touched the dockworkers' pendants with an implement rather like a small flashlight, apparently in payment. He held my pendant for a moment before shrugging and paying me, too.

I approached the hovercraft driver.

"Is the third level going to be late?" I asked.

"Oh, yes. I hope blood will be spilled," he said.

"You could tell me to get in with the cargo to make sure none of it shifts," I said. "It wouldn't hurt to have a witness to confirm that she gave exact orders about how to stow the items."

"Are you sure?" he asked. "You'll end up at the Capital."

"That's where I want to go," I said.

17

He shrugged. "It's your funeral. Hop on board."

As the hovercraft rose from the dock, I heard Ky give the limo driver grief as he returned to his vehicle.

The buildings along the route looked old and ill-kept. I wondered if we would have to go over a gigantic mountain in front of us. As we got closer, I saw the mountain was actually a multi-story building shaped like the spaceship that landed on earth. The road split into multiple lanes that led to various entrances. Vehicles of all kinds idled bumper to bumper on every route.

"I'm late, you miserable excuse for a tree swinger," Ky screamed at the driver. "Take the road to the main entrance and let me off before you unload. You don't merit an actual challenge, but I promise you're going to regret this."

The vehicle must have been familiar to the Razor guards. They waved us through three gates before we had to stop. At the fourth stop, a Razor jumped into the cargo bed. Before I was able to react, he picked me up and tossed me over the side.

"Wai—!" I shouted. My jujutsu training kicked in. I twisted my body like a gymnast trying to stick a landing, but another Razor on the ground kicked me in the stomach while I was still in midair. Pain shot through me. My lungs expelled air. I slammed onto the road on my hands and knees. The impact was hard, like a car crash. Jolts of electric pain flew through my hips, elbows, and shoulders as I slid along the roadway, shredding my knees and my palms. Losing momentum, I collapsed face down. Then I curled into the fetal position.

A guard put his fine-edged outer forearm against my throat. "Tell me why I shouldn't kill you," he demanded.

CHAPTER FIVE

Matter of—
I gasped.
—of honor.
Through the disorienting pain and the sense of panic that I was going to die, I managed to slow my breathing.

"A matter of honor," I spat out Jimmy's words.
Stay submissive. Stay submissive.

"Your species has no honor. You are too miserable to bother with. You cannot be dishonored."

I froze. I had to say this right or he would kill me. "Not me." I took another breath. "A Plix... dishonored... one of her own kind."

The guard hesitated. I began to think I might live a little longer if I managed to gather my wits and speak coherently.

"I was a witness. I thought Razors valued honor enough to want to know when it is tarnished."

I was too frightened to give voice to my afterthought: *Or maybe not.*

The guard moved his forearm an inch away from the artery pounding in my neck.

I took a breath. I felt sweat streaming from my temples. I looked at my hands. They were a bloody mess.

The guard glanced to his right and then looked back at me, where I cowered in his shadow. Neither he nor I spoke. That's how we stayed for several minutes, till a being rather like a mutated two-legged bloodhound approached.

The guard shook me. "Speak," he demanded.

The being closed its eyes.

"A Plix— dishonored one of her own kind," I said again, more forcefully this time.

"Well?" the guard asked the other alien.

The being opened its eyes. "By his smell I can tell that he speaks truly."

The guard kicked at me and grumbled, "Get up. Follow me."

I limped in his wake into the Capital. Three other guards came with us and four more guards took their places. Inside, beings moved rapidly on errands I did not understand. Most were Razors, but there were others in physical forms beyond my dreams and nightmares that crawled, flew, and slid along the corridors.

The guard knocked on a door. When it opened from the inside, I saw a smaller, fatter Razor seated behind an ordinary-looking desk. He waved me in. All four guards filed in behind me and surrounded me as I stood a few feet from the desk.

"Tell me about Ky," said the seated Razor.

Ky must have wasted no time in shouting out her complaints. I wondered if the Plix ambassador was aware yet of any damage to his possessions. I was tempted to leave out information about how the driver and I set her up, but the small Razor had an aura about him that made me think better of it. Keeping my eyes down, I told him in detail from the beginning what had happened.

"Did she enter the order into the record for where the material was to be packed?" asked the Razor.

I paused, thinking it was essential to be precise in my answers.

"I don't know for certain, sir. I overheard her say that she had. Of course, I did not see what she did. In fact, I never saw her in person."

The alien stared at me. He touched one pearl-colored button on a row of buttons built into the desk.

"Stop the execution of that ape driver. Put him back in his cell," he said aloud. There was a clicking sound, and then he looked again at me.

"I find it hard to believe that you came here just to testify about

Ky, annoying as she is."

"That was one reason," I said. "You're right, sir. There was another reason."

"Why? I'm curious. I've never seen an alien like you before. There are easier ways to commit suicide."

I pulled my pendant out from under my shirt and held it out toward him.

"You want to get paid? Okay."

He reached for the payment mechanism.

"No, sir," I said. "My word is not for sale. I don't want anything for testifying. I wanted to show you this key."

He ignored the key, drummed his fingers on his desk, and then tapped the same button he had pushed before.

"I have confirmed the ape driver's account. Let him go."

He looked at me again. "I believe you. If you wanted money for your account, you'd tell the story to support Ky.

An honest alien. Imagine that."

I pointed to the key. "Sir, with respect, I believe this object is proof that I am the ambassador from the planet we call Earth."

"Maybe so," said the alien. "I've never seen one like it before."

"Well, I'm an ambassador so I am here legally, sir," I said. "If I may ask, aren't there certain protections and rights accorded to ambassadors, no matter where they're from?"

"Probably, but I'm a simple watch commander. I don't have any idea what they are."

"I apologize abjectly of my complete ignorance about such matters, sir. Perhaps you might contact someone who could assist me in my new role," I said.

With an expression that might have been a half-smile, he leaned toward me and said, "No doubt I could. Why should I trouble myself to do so?"

I had to keep his interest.

"Kindness?" I asked.

He gave a short laugh.

"Curiosity?"

"Hmmm."

"One tiny scrap of respect, then, sir," I said. "I believe I am the first Earth Ambassador to actually make it to the Capital. Watch Commander, sir, you have shown absolute fairness in listening to me despite my species. You have been strictly professional with me, which I greatly appreciate. I hope I have been adequately respectful toward you." I bowed a bow that felt a little over the top.

He paused. My heart pounded. I felt like I might faint. He looked at me for a moment that seemed to last for hours. He shrugged. Then he pressed a different button on his desk. "Ask a fully vetted steward to come to my office. There is a situation that requires attention and knowledge I do not possess."

He turned to me.

"How did my guards perform with you?"

"These guards observed that I was an unknown person. They rendered me helpless with total efficiency but they did not kill me, which would have caused the loss of whatever information I might have. Instead, they assessed the situation correctly and brought me here. I thought they did well. If I may make an additional observation without sounding offensive or critical?"

He nodded his head.

"These guards are from the fourth gate," I said. "The guards at the first three gates allowed me to pass unchallenged."

"That's information worth paying for, Earthman." He reached for his payment implement, motioned me to hold my pendant closer to him, and touched it to the stone on the pendant. "I knew it, of course, but it was worth my while to have it verified and to find out that you recognized the situation."

The chain moved on its own.

"What the— ?" I blurted. The chain around my neck became longer and thicker as I watched. Its color changed to silver. The pendant also changed from cheap metal to what looked like pewter. The gravel stone morphed into quartz with black veins running through it.

The alien chuckled. "You're coming up in society. As your wealth increases, your necklace will reflect it." A shimmering silver screen rose from the desk. Colors bloomed and then faded on my side of the screen. The Razor sat in silence, while he scanned his side.

"You're Liam Conner. Interesting history. Yes, you are the first Earth Ambassador to show up in the Capital. Hmm. An honest alien who survived all the way here. It might be interesting to see how long you can stay alive."

"If you don't mind telling me, who are you, sir?" I asked. I took a breath and continued, "Sir, I find it hard to believe that a simple watch commander can dictate the outcome of a trial and call a steward to come see me."

"My name is Fez. I am currently the watch commander that evaluates rumors of problems with the guards, which you confirmed. I have a variety of administrative roles. As a member of the royal family, I have certain privileges, such as facilitating the entry of a person into our society who might shake things up. We have become too comfortable and complacent in our ways."

"I doubt, Your Grace, that I will stay alive long enough to do much of that," I answered. "Surely, you're aware that my cancer will kill me soon."

"Your Grace. I like that title," he said. "I'll have to remember that. You obviously didn't understand what your universal translator told you. We Razors don't accept damaged merchandise. Your captain was told to nullify your cancer while you were in transit, and he did."

My knees buckled. I dropped to the floor. One death sentence had been lifted. The Razors were still likely to kill me anyway, but knowing the cancer was over was a relief. Chemotherapy had been horrendous. I'd take a pill, feel fairly decent, and then when the medicine kicked in, I felt like I was falling off a cliff. I had headaches that hurt so badly I felt like my skull had split open. Once, I became convinced that a dream about a baby meant a real baby was in danger. I knew intellectually that a dream figure was not real, but my emotions spiked despite that. For some time while I was hospitalized, I saw demons in neon red and green every time I closed my eyes.

"Interesting biological response," said Fez. "I suspect that was an evolutionary advance."

"So, my cancer is gone?" I asked timidly.

"Apparently entirely. Don't ask me about the cure. I don't understand how it's done. Don't embarrass yourself by expressing gratitude to me. There was nothing personal in the regulations. You fell under the general category for transporting biological items like fresh fruit."

A taller creature that resembled the Razors, except that it was the color of ripe wheat, entered the room. It had a much larger abdomen and thinner antennae compared to the guards and Fez. From my study of the praying mantis on Earth I suspected that this was a female.

"How may I be assistance, Watch Commander?" it asked.

"The thing on the floor is Liam Conner, Earth Ambassador. I believe we are supposed to provide it with food and lodgings and so forth. I am not acquainted with the protocols for newly arrived representatives. Take it to an appropriate place and provide it with a general orientation to the Capital."

The steward's expression changed to what I guessed was displeasure. Alien facial expressions were surprisingly close to those of humans. She pulled a small device out of her coverings. After tapping on buttons, a screen lit up. I held up the key. She looked from the screen to the key and back again.

"It has the correct implement. It is the Ambassador. We reserved a placeholder for humans when they became your clients, but there will have to be some major changes to accommodate it. At present, we are in a state of disarray and dwindling numbers. I suppose I can house it in a unit marginally suited to an ambassador after the bodies are removed from the premises and the walls and floors mopped up. The location is close to the Plix embassy offices and residences. I have been waiting for the tumult to subside before starting the disinfecting to be efficient."

"Would that put it in immediate danger?" asked Fez. "What is your name?"

"I am Laa, at your service, Honored One. Yes, I think it would be easiest to wait for its demise, which should be soon. After the discord is over, the whole area can be sanitized."

"Thank you for your concern for the collective, Laa. I am pleased that you have the well-being of Razors in mind. So many of the other species who work under our benign care put their species ahead of my family. However, I have a certain curiosity about this

24

earthman, Conner. I want it alive long enough to observe its interactions with us."

"Of course. I can have its quarters thoroughly cleaned and set up a support staff, if you like. It will be near the Plix, so who knows what events coming from that chaos may cause its termination? If you will permit me a short time to set preparations in action, sir."

She stepped outside the office. Fez ignored me as he returned to his duties. I noted the guards remained on their feet and alert, constantly looking around. I was content to sit silently on the floor.

"Jimmy, what do you think?"

I think Laa is not happy that she can't just sluff you off to her murderous friends. This is much longer than I expected you and I to stay alive. Others of my species are excited. They are taking notes.

"If they have thoughts or suggestions, please let me know."

They say that legally the Captain was only obliged to stabilize your cancer. He eliminated it entirely. He liked you.

"I wonder if I can pay him to share the treatment with Earth doctors. Imagine if there was an actual benefit to having the Razors as sponsors."

Laa returned to the room.

"Honored One, I have made the arrangements."

"Good. The guards will accompany you. Hy is the sergeant."

I caught a fleeting glimpse of what I thought was dismay on Laa's face.

More guards awaited us outside Fez's office. One guard took a position behind Laa and Hy. Two other guards walked on each side of me. The last took his place behind me. Beings gave our diamond-shaped group plenty of room as we walked. Wide-bodied aliens squeezed to the side and halted as we passed.

After two hundred feet or so of progress, a Plix approaching us hesitated and then strode straight toward Laa. By stopping a yard short of us, he blocked our movements. Then he looked right at me.

"Lying Earth Ambassador, I challenge you," he called.

CHAPTER SIX

The guards moved close around me. I broke out in a sweat, wondering if my deliverance from cancer was a lousy cosmic joke. I took a breath to gather my thoughts and keep my voice level.

"Please forgive my ignorance," I said, keeping my head down. "I just arrived. I don't understand what you are talking about or the significance of your statement."

"Ignorant simian, I am Wyn. I am challenging you to a duel to the death in the Arena because of your lies." Thrusting his shoulders back and his chest forward, he struck a fighting pose.

"I am the Earth Ambassador. I don't l know what lies you imagine I made."

"The lies about Ky."

"Ah, that helps me understand. You were misinformed. I told no lies about her. And I have never seen you before, sir," I explained, still avoiding looking directly at him. "You weren't present when I spoke to the Watch Commander. If you don't mind me asking, how do you know what, if anything, I said?"

"I was told what you said."

"By whom, sir? I haven't told you. Was it the Watch Commander or the guards here? Nobody else was present."

"You accuse me of lying or you accuse Ky."

"Not at all." I gave a small bow. "I have no reason to think you or Ky lied. However, I don't understand how your informant could possibly give you accurate information."

I looked at the guards. "Without getting into the details of what was said, did any of you hear me accuse anyone of lying?"

Each said no.

Wyn's shoulders began to sag.

"Do you expect me to apologize to a lowly human?" Wyn demanded.

"Of course not," I answered, trying to stay calm. "You reacted honorably to what you believed to be true. You have nothing to apologize for. However, what you believed is not what happened." I felt like I was trying to play a tune using only one note.

Wyn rocked back and forth from foot to foot. "I cannot retract my challenge. That would imply an inferior corrected a Plix. The guards must be lying for you." He jumped toward me.

Propelled by a quick thrust of Hy's arm, I went flying to the left. The rest of the guards rushed into action. Even before I landed, Wyn's body fell to the floor, sliced and oozing blood in half a dozen places. I managed to roll through my landing, ending up several feet away from the starting point.

"Congratulations," said Hy. "He challenged you to a duel. That suggests you are no longer beneath notice. You are acquiring status. Naturally, you don't have the right to actually fight in the Arena. And no simian can compete with an insectoid. He should have just assassinated you.

Switch of status. Now I had to initiate dominance. I had to become the hammer, not the anvil. I took a deep breath and turned toward Laa.

"Give me one really good reason I should not ask for your execution. The guards can march you back to the Honored One immediately so you can explain your treachery to him."

She froze.

"I might be just an 'it' to you, but I am not a stupid 'it.' Who knew about Ky and the route we would take? Who had the chance to set up this ambush? Only you."

"Ky is my sister," she hissed, apparently uncertain how to react to a being without status who was making a serious accusation. "Fez can order the deaths of all who came from our egg sack and all other descendants of our maternal family. Dozens could die."

"So, what's that to me?" I snapped. "Why should I care?"

"I'll never betray you again, Conner."

This was different – hearing a Plix say my name.

"If I take you back to Fez and ask him to kill you, the next steward will be too scared to try anything. Now that you speak my name, I will give you one last chance to save your life. I know absolutely nothing about your culture. You can help me survive. Make me the best possible offer, and maybe I will ask Fez to lessen the punishment and allow your bloodline to continue."

Laa looked away. She was quiet for several seconds. When she spoke, her voice quavered.

"I offer you nothing, ape. I stumbled across an antiquated law while I was researching property rights. A person who has greatly disgraced herself can voluntarily cede all personal rights and property to an authority. The rights and property holder can then demand her suicide at any moment. All demands must be met with instant obedience. Blood relatives must contribute monetarily to the person's owner for all expenses incurred at a rate determined by the authority."

"That sounds like slavery," I asked. "On earth, it was abolished centuries ago, although remnants of that abomination still stain morality in my country."

"The request does not have to be accepted," she said. "No one has made it for several generations. To protect my family, I will make the offer to Fez. To you, as I said, I offer nothing, you— you mammalian. You simian. You ape."

Head held high, she led us back to Fez's office. When he told us to come in, Laa knelt before him. She described her disobedience in exquisite detail before citing the ancient law and offering herself to him in complete surrender.

"What do you think, Conner?" he asked.

"I am in no position to judge or advise you, sir," I said. "Personally, I could not bring myself to own another person. We outlawed slavery in my country centuries ago."

Fez clenched his jaw and frowned. "So, you think your planet is more advanced than mine about this?"

Damn. Had I already forgotten my practice at begging? Fez was infinitely superior to me, in his mind anyway. I was going to get myself steamrolled if I didn't do this right.

Fez looked at Laa, still on her knees. "This law you cling to is a terrible one that should be stricken from the books, but it holds a certain fascination for me. Laa, despite your betrayal, I find myself reluctant to deprive the Collective of your creatively twisted mind."

He paused, glancing at me for a moment before resuming his explanation. "I certainly cannot refrain from severe punishment. And allowing you to kill yourself would be much too lenient. Your family has grown too arrogant, too rich, and too disrespectful. I accept your plea. Only ten percent of your mother's offspring will be killed, while their assets, and all of yours, of course, will be sent to my personal account. You will assist and advise Conner in any way he chooses. When he dies, you will die. Should he at any time express dissatisfaction with your services, you plus another forty percent of your family will be terminated. Is that clear?"

"Yes, sir," she croaked.

"Conner, I suppose your disdain for owning people is part of your primitive cultural heritage. You may refuse to accept her, but then I shall be forced to suspend my generosity. She and seventy-five percent of her family will be destroyed."

Laa gasped.

I grimaced, my head reeling.

Fez continued, "In return for your acceptance, I will have, oh, two, no, three percent of the seized family assets assigned to you. What do you say?"

I hesitated for a heartbeat and swallowed. I felt trapped and cursed myself for abandoning my position of total submission. All I could do was to not make things worse.

"As you wish, sir." I bowed deeply.

"A most interesting afternoon," Fez murmured. "Be gone."

This time, as we moved through the corridors, Laa walked next to me and told the guard in the lead when to turn.

"For an intelligent Plix, your plan seems seriously flawed," I said to her as we entered a new hallway. "Why would anyone have believed my death was an accident?"

"It wouldn't matter what people believed," she said. "A dead witness under questionable circumstances would have given room for all sorts of rumors about conspiracies. In the Capital, the most unlikely and convoluted explanation is likely to be the correct one. How could I have anticipated Fez would bother with you and pay attention to a passing quarrel in the hallways? He's probably the only royal who would bother."

"I suppose when Fez ordered the guards to come with us it was too late to call it off," I said. "But Wyn had to know the whole thing was unraveling. He might have backed off with no loss of prestige. Why did he attack?"

"To back away would have resulted in questions that would eventually lead to me," she said. "He was ensnared, and death was preferable to betrayal."

"It was? Why?"

"Why do you think?" she spat out.

"I have no clue," I answered.

Laa shifted her eyes and looked at me. "You really are a simpleton. Wyn thought there was a chance he would have sex with me. I have substantially more social status than he did. He was not about to abandon the possible prestige he would gain. He was noted for his constant bragging about his sexual prowess. Surely it is the same on your pathetic planet."

"Sometimes," I said. "It is not totally unknown."

Laa grunted. "It is particularly humiliating that I will now be forced to submit to your sexual urges. It is a perversion worse than everything else to couple with a lower lifeform."

"I see," I said. "Why go to such a risk to defend your sister?"

"My conniving bitch of a sister puts my entire bloodline at risk by her petulant actions. If she had groveled and wept instead of protesting and blaming the insignificant transport driver, she would probably have been the only one killed. I don't care about her. I hoped to limit the consequences to my family."

She looked at me eye to eye. "In that I was successful, human. You did not defeat me."

"I tried to survive," I said. "In that I was successful. Each of us achieved our respective goals. We are not in competition. Cooperation with me is the best thing you can do for your lineage now. I am more interested in survival than in vengeance."

"Shameless barbarian," she said. "You have no name, no honor, and no value. You know less than a nymph. Still, I will work with you, ape, as long as it is in my interest to do so."

"Good. So tell me about Fez. What is his position in the royal family? Who outranks him?"

"He is a member of the family. That is enough," she said.

I knew that I had to establish a relationship that would maximize my chances to stay alive in this hostile place. I saw no way to turn her into an ally so I had to adopt the morals of the planet. I had to make it clear that, despite my species, I was the alpha in our relationship.

"That is not an acceptable answer. I can get that information from your replacement," I told her, pausing for effect. "I need more from you than truthful information. I need context. I need you to tell me what I don't know enough to ask about. As you said, I am more ignorant than a hatchling. If you do not give me comprehensive and complete information, you will be no more useful than a replacement would be. And you will be a problem I can live without. No matter how charming you and your sister have been, I will not hesitate to ask Fez to end your existence when you become more trouble than you are worth."

She stopped. I continued walking, ignoring her. After a moment, she hurried after me.

"Listen to me, Laa. I don't care what you call me when we are alone, but when there are others around you will refer to me as Ambassador, sir, or Conner. You will act with the appearance of respect. I don't give a damn what your actual opinion of me is. Now, answer my question."

Laa looked from side to side before she replied in a soft voice, "Conner, it is not wise to talk about the royal family in a public place. They have spies everywhere. People who aren't spies are rewarded for sharing what people say about them. The family is secretive about who outranks whom. Fez is younger than many in the family, but he is unusually active in making decisions. He sometimes retracts his judgments, but it is not clear if someone told him to change his mind or if he did it on his own. There have to be disagreements from time to time, but the family presents itself as always unified."

"That's the sort of thing I need to know," I said. "Is my personal residence ready for my arrival?"

"No, sir. Uh, I did not expect you to ever get there. I set up the appointment with the Plix Ambassador for you, but only in case Fez would check with him."

"What needs to be done to get my embassy ready?"

"The setting has been renovated but there are no staff, no butler, guards, hunter, or domestics. Obviously, you will need a new wardrobe, consumables, and furnishings. The Collective will cover the expenses. I was waiting to see who would occupy the dwelling."

"Well, Laa, now we know who will live there, don't we? I also want to consult with a doctor who has worked with humanoids."

"With whom?"

"Apes, Laa. Simians. Mammalians. Start hiring. You can do everything needed until the staff is on board. And I want to meet with someone at the Arena."

"You wouldn't last an eyeblink in a duel at the Arena, Ambassador."

"Truly."

"It will not be easy to find a chef who knows about the weeds you eat and how to char flesh," said Laa. "I don't know why your kind won't kill and eat your fresh kill at meals like we do. I suppose someone prepares meals for apes, but I don't know who."

...

We arrived at would quickly become the Earth Embassy. The building occupied space equivalent to a skyscraper New York hotel. The activity at the entrances was like that of an anthill as workers carried in supplies, furniture, and appliances, or what looked like appliances.

I asked the guards if they wanted to leave. They said they would wait until I was settled. Hy agreed to interview potential security personnel. Laa said she would interview beings for open positions.

Along the outside walls of the building was a long line of beings, waiting for something. I saw a list of open positions posted on a door. As Laa peeled away and walked to a desk, I realized that these were potential workers. She wasted no time in interviewing the first being in line.

While I watched and waited in the chaos around me, I was approached by a chubby Plix and a fleet of attendants. Over a lacy eggplant-purple leisure suit he wore a flowing robe that Moses would have envied. His attendants were dressed less colorfully and were decidedly thinner.

The guards saw him and seemed relaxed.

"Conner, I believe," he said.

"Yes, sir. I regret that I don't know who you are."

He waved his hand. "Nobody important. I am Gi, humble Plix Ambassador to the Razor Collective."

I thought his choice of clothing implied anything except humility. And he was the first alien to go out of the way to meet me. I played along to find out what he wanted.

"I'm glad to see you are safe, sir," I said. "Apparently, there have been some deaths of embassy staff."

"Oh, the rumors are greatly exaggerated. You see, back on the home planet there has been a conflict for thousands of years between my lineage and Ky's family. Her family achieved temporary religious and political gains from some very unfortunate and unwise decisions by certain distant relatives of mine in the government. She was sent to see if similar irregularities had taken place here. Of course, they had not."

I nodded, thinking Gi would have fit in perfectly in the Gunderson administration.

"I'm afraid Ky demonstrated the arrogance and mental instability that occurs so frequently in that brilliant but high-strung bloodline. She was exceedingly tardy and disrespectful toward the rest of my hard-working staff. Then she was blatantly dishonest by trying to blame a stupid ape driver for crushing valuable imports belonging to her superiors."

"Oh, is that what happened?" I asked. He ignored my mock-innocent tone of voice and plowed ahead.

"Yes. The driver and the low-life dock workers were no doubt out of line. What can you expect from lesser species? But she ordered her possessions to placed exactly where they would do the most damage to everyone else's luggage."

"Unbelievable selfishness," I said.

Just like the Ambassador himself.

"And needlessly spiteful," added Gi. He peered over my shoulder. "There are rumors that her sister has been actively opposing the wishes of the royal family, and, although it is hard to believe, is now indentured to, well, to you."

Ah, now we were getting to the purpose of his visit.

"Wow. Rumors spread faster than wildfire here," I said. "Like you, I'm sure, I do not gossip about the royal family. But since you were kind enough to ask, look over there."

"Oh, my goodness. It is Laa. And has she been ordered to assist you in any way you choose?"

"I believe that is correct," I said.

"Conner, it is crucial that you understand the circumstances exactly. It would be terrible to overstep your authority. I can check on that for you."

"That is kind of you," I said, although since he already knew the situation, he clearly had time to find out the relevant information.

"I shall do it gladly," said Gi. "She has no doubt already propositioned you. You have to be very careful with females in her family. Reportedly, they mate willingly with anything with a penis. Their madness is rumored to stoke their passion. They excrete extremely powerful pheromones and can gain control of a male by that means." He stared at Laa and his smile widened. I expected him to start drooling at any moment.

"Uh, thank you, Gi. Can I call you Gi?"

"Well, I don't usually allow substantially lesser beings to.... Why, yes, of course. We are both Ambassadors. We reside in the same area. I will grant you the liberty of using my name. Understand, if she is truly indentured, you have the rights to her sexual favors."

"Really?" I asked. I suspected what was coming next.

"Oh, yes. After you satisfy yourself, you can decide to share those favors with others. I mean, of course, for a reasonable price. It can be quite lucrative. Oh, that reminds me." He reached into his robe and brought out a small flashlight-like implement identical to what the dock straw boss and Fez held.

34

"Your interactions with Fez resulted in making my life much easier, not to mention safer. A quarter of my staff has been eliminated."

"I'm sorry."

"Not at all, Conner. That quarter was disloyal, including everyone I suspected. And a few I wasn't aware that were backstabbers. It is only fair that I reward you for our services, even if you were not conscious of your assistance to me. It was unwieldy to supervise so many people. I suggest you limit your people to as few as possible."

I took the silver chain off my neck and handed it to him. When he touched the payment-giving device to the necklace, it expanded and changed from silver to gold. The links thickened and became a series of figure eights. The pendant became white gold. The stone morphed into a delicate shade of blue. The transformation seemed like magic. I blinked and stared at it.

"A sky-blue topaz. It's not particularly valuable, but it's pretty, isn't it?" he asked.

Gi was about as subtle as a blackjack to the base of the skull. He had money to burn and I had what he wanted. I'd had many dirty jobs over the years, like mucking out barns and unclogging sewers, but I had never been a pimp. I had no desire to add that job title to my resume. I think something in my thoughts showed in my face.

Gi took a step backward. "I must return now," he said. "The work of an Ambassador is never done."

I relaxed and smiled at him.

"Speaking of ambassadors, sir, can I ask you if I should I notify the royal family formally that I have arrived? Should I ask for an audience, or what?"

"Oh, no. I don't know about customs on your planet. The role of an ambassador on this world is to represent your species when they conflict with the Razor authorities, for the convenience of the Razors, of course. Asking them to spend their precious time with your concerns would be considered highly presumptuous." He sniffed.

"Thank you, sir. May I ask from curiosity, Gi, how often do you see the royal family?"

"I have only been Ambassador for two decades. I'm told I was on the alternate list to attend an event at least twice. My predecessor was invited to a ceremony where two members of the family were actually present."

"Oh, my," I said.

"Yes, I am most proud of that. I will do the research and inform you of my findings."

"Thank you for your kindness," I said. "It was most instructive to meet you." Half of my statement was true.

I watched as he and his attendants walked away.

"Jimmy, you are supposed to help me keep my cool, not encourage me toward putting a-holes in their place."

Sorry, Conner.

CHAPTER SEVEN

When I turned my attention back to the activities going on, a creature approached me who had the approximate form of a four-foot walking amber-colored octopus.

"You must be Conner. I can't tell you how exciting it is to meet a human. My hobby is studying animal life on Earth, including your species in particular, with its mythology and history. I am particularly taken with a sea creature that looks like a distant relative of mine."

"The octopus," I said. "They are quite intelligent and they lead interesting, if short, lives. But you probably know more about them than I do."

"Yes. Have you seen one?"

"Yes. I touched one in an aquarium once. What little I have learned about them is fascinating. Do you think there is any biological overlap between their species and yours?"

"I would love to find out. You can call me Doc. If you come with me to a quiet room inside your embassy, I can do an examination and give you something for your contusions and bruises if my female gender does not bother you."

"Sure. Let me tell the guards where I will be."

"Yes, you'll want their assurance that I am not a danger to you."

The guards were bantering with some tough-looking characters when I approached them. They waved me and Doc through into the building.

In a private room, I disrobed while Doc looked me over. She spoke with Jimmy in technical terms I didn't understand. She gently took some cells by swabbing inside my mouth and gave me an ointment to use on my scraped skin.

"From the limited study I've made of human medicine, I would say you have unusually fast reflexes, flexibility, and strength for a male of your age. I can leave you pills to thin the walls of your circulation system, restore decreased cushioning of your joints, and lessen the size of your prostate. Other medications will also improve flexibility, skin elasticity, grip, memory retrieval, and so forth to correct the effects of aging. You have a number of old bone fractures that have healed nicely. Apparently, you are active in a sport, which you should continue. There is no evidence of cancer."

"That's good to hear."

"With additional medication, you should be able to regain the strength and short-term memory capacity you had during your prime. Do you have any questions?"

"Yes, Doc. Could you share medical information developments you have if I had a way to communicate it to Earth? I mean, I would pay you for that service, of course. It would advance medical practice considerably."

"Possibly, but we have a strict policy of noninterference with developing planets. The search for information about one thing often leads to discovering other things along the way. However, I will consider the question. Anything else?"

"Yes. Is Laa pumping out an unusual amount of pheromone?"

"Yes, I noticed that. The mating practices of insectoids on Razor Prime are somewhat like the Earth mythology surrounding Spartan women. The women were well-educated and excelled at sports. There was a myth that a man would try to kidnap a woman and force her sexually in order to marry her. She would fight back and vanquish men she did not like, proving them unworthy of her. Females here are strong and independent. Laa would respect a male who can match her intelligence and equal her competence in wordplay. She is stronger and quicker than you are due to your different biology, but I believe she has met only a few males who can compete with her in other areas. At least I can assure you that Plix females do not eat their mates as many Earth insects who resemble them do."

"Can Laa use her pheromones to influence males?" I asked.

"Of course. Don't human women use their attractiveness for their own goals with human men? Laa is putting a great deal of the chemical out. It is as if she were in danger of dying and needs to influence a male in a final effort to try to stay alive."

"That must be what she's doing," I said. "She persuaded one male to try to kill me. Then she pled for her life with another one."

"As insectoids, their reactions would be greater than yours," said Doc. "I doubt that pheromones cross species boundaries easily. With so much going on, she would have trouble shutting it off. Her body might still be pumping out the implied sexual invitation."

"And I was told that Plix women who have sex with a male gain greater control over him."

"I suppose it might be true," said Doc. "Or it might not. Right now, she is indentured to you. I suppose it is possible she wants to persuade you to keep her alive by using her pheromones. You can, of course, demand her sexual favors. Her humiliation would be extreme."

"I will never do that. I've never forced myself on a woman. I'm not about to start now. Please tell her. I don't want to upset her by bringing the subject up. She might think I was tormenting her or lying."

"I believe you. That's good to know. In that case, if you like, I will become your physician."

"Thank you. I would like that."

Outside the building, I walked up to Laa. I stepped between her and the being she was in an intense conversation with.

"What?" she demanded.

"Are the basic staff for food and housekeeping hired?"

"More or less, but I have many more people to talk with."

"Wrap it up for today. I'll hire security and we'll shut it down until tomorrow. Then get inside and stop putting out pheromones. Look at the crowd. The males are getting hostile toward each other. We're going to have fights breaking out if you keep it up. Ten minutes until lockdown."

She looked ready to bite my head off until she looked at the unruly and growing crowd. Her facial features relaxed.

"Fifteen minutes," she said.

"Ten. I don't want any riots on my first day as Ambassador."

I walked over to the guards and thanked each one individually for what he specifically had done that day. Then I turned to Hy.

"Okay, Hy, who can I trust who has crowd control and fighting skills?"

It turned out that one of the local street gangs with twenty members had family ties with the guards. The members were Plix and Razors, with a few ape-based aliens thrown in. Most were males, but a few were females.

"They can do the job but they're not polished and polite," said Hy.

"Well neither am I."

I called out, "Gather 'round. Does anybody have a problem working for an ugly, smelly alien who has thin skin, no teeth worth mentioning, and no claws or sharp edges on his body? I am a tiny hatchling and you can put me down in seconds. But, make no mistake, I am the physically insignificant creature who's the boss. Anybody want out?"

I waited as they looked at each other and shrugged.

"Okay, five of you stop anyone else from entering the building," I said. "Three teams of five of you need to go floor to floor, chasing out everybody in the building, no matter who they are or what they're doing. After the building is emptied, Laa or I will approve each person allowed to enter. After that, a few of you at a time can go get your stuff, get something to eat, and then move into rooms on the first floor. I want four guards on eight-hour shifts for now. One rotating backup per shift. You work out the schedule, who heads each shift, and who your officers are."

One young male Razor sauntered toward me. He spat on my shoe. "How much do we get paid? Do you really think you can tell a Razor what to do? I might consider signing up, if I would be the boss."

I wasn't surprised. A low-status mammal commanding insectoids? Still, it was clear that he was testing me. I looked at the guards. They looked alert and ready. I winked at Hy and turned toward the

40

smart aleck.

"When I want questions or comments from idiots, I'll let you know," I said. "One team will have only four members until we get a replacement for this jackass."

The Razor jumped at me, knocking me to the ground.

...

I groaned. When I opened my eyes, Ye, a Plix and one of the new Embassy guards who was also the former gang leader, was sitting in a chair next to my bed.

"Welcome back to the land of the living."

"How long have I been out?" I asked. "What happened?"

"You weren't out long, about ten seconds. Doc examined you, gave you something to inhale, and said to take you inside and let you sleep. You slept about two hours, and now you're awake."

I took a moment to assess the aches in my back and arms. "So, what am I missing? What didn't I see?"

"Qa surprised the guards by attacking so quickly. Laa jumped to stand over your body. She exchanged insults with Qa. Nobody in his right mind will mess with a female Plix in heat. Are you two mating?"

"No. That won't happen. Hey, I don't have a headache or dizziness. I've been knocked unconscious in fights and I never felt this good afterward, but I don't remember anything after I fell. Qa knocked me out?"

"You hit your head on a rock. Hy sends his apologies. He said he didn't understand your signal."

"Damn, that was my fault," I said. "I assumed he would know something was about to happen. I should have explained my plan. Whatever Doc gave me was amazingly effective. What happened to Qa?"

"Hy kicked his ass all over the place," said Ye. "Qa ran away like a cockroach caught by a searchlight. He backed down to Laa and then to Hy. Qa lost everybody's respect. He always wanted to be the gang leader. He pushed for us to do exciting, dangerous things. Some of the younger gang members thought he would make a good

41

leader. And he's a Razor, which he thinks makes him special. Qa is bound to attack you personally now to end his disgrace. You'll have to watch your back constantly."

I had not intended to make a determined enemy. My carelessness nearly killed me. How many mistakes would I survive?

CHAPTER EIGHT

Whatever medication Doc gave me healed the scrapes and bruises. I had new pink skin without scabs where there had been contusions. Jimmy walked me through taking a shower and using the bathroom. I found a clean robe, sweatpants, and sandals in a closet. The sandals did not give me the stability I wanted, so I chose the work boots I had worn before.

I walked downstairs. Jimmy directed me to a room with a window that showed a quiet outside scene. I stopped a passing Plix I did not recall seeing before.

"I would like you to bring me something to eat, and please tell Laa to join me."

The Plix looked me up and down before replying, "Why should I do that? I have things to do. Laa said she should not be bothered with minor details."

"How long have you been working here?" I asked.

"About three hours."

"What's your name?"

"I am Ef, second-level assistant to Laa."

"Ef, if you would like to continue your employment for four hours, you will follow my instructions immediately. Tell Laa when you see her that the Ambassador will see her. Now go."

Ef scurried away. I reminded myself to stop being polite. Laa had apparently hired enough basic staff members to allow the Embassy to function, although I was far from certain what the function of the place was supposed to be. I represented the human population on Razor Prime, and I was the entire human population on the planet. My job performance had been lousy so far. I had to keep up the air of superiority. Otherwise, I would be inferior. This world did not recognize much in the middle.

Laa soon arrived carrying a plate of vegetables and the Razor version of a fork.

"Did you have to scare my new assistant?" she asked.

"I didn't have to, but she encouraged me to by her attitude. Inform your staff that it is not wise to assume they are more important than somebody else, no matter how insignificant and odd that somebody looks. Especially when that somebody might be me." I dug into the food.

Laa watched without comment.

"Thanks for standing over me and protecting me after I passed out," I said between bites.

"Your death would result in my death," she said. "By the way, eating weeds like a domesticated cow is disgusting."

I waved off the comment.

"How is the embassy coming along?" I asked.

"I got much of the hiring done while you were not around to bother me. The building has been sanitized. I presume you will want considerable remodeling to make it more suitable to your needs. We need to talk about that. I had serious doubts about hiring a street gang as security, but they are surprisingly loyal to you. They question everyone who tries to enter and follow anyone that they don't know and ask me who the strangers are."

I nodded. She continued. "Ambassador Gi sent an urgent message saying his research confirmed what he expected. You are invited to drop by his embassy with me in tow at any time. I don't understand what his message is about. I'm surprised he even acknowledges your existence. He is obsessive about status and privilege, like the rest of his ridiculous family. The people at the Arena said you are free to go there to see the Master, but they would not set up an appointment. You can go there, but you might have to wait quite a while until he is free."

"Excellent. For your information, Ambassador Gi suggested that since you are indentured to me, I can rent you out for sexual favors. I assume he means to him."

"Fat bastard," she snarled. "I should have guessed from the way he looked at me."

"That's not going to happen," I said. "Not ever."

Laa relaxed her posture.

"I'd like to meet with a tailor and cobbler to get a new wardrobe and better shoes. Don't throw out the clothes I had on. Have them washed and patched if they need it. I would like to get new clothes from one of the little shops close by. For that matter, I want us to buy food locally to support businesses around here. I understand how it feels to barely scrape by. I'll meet with the guards later. What else? Doc is remarkable. I think I'll take some bodyguards and go to the Arena now. I will probably be there for some time. Unless you see a reason to accompany me, I'd like you to stay here and continue what you're doing."

"Go. Then I can get some work done. Try not to intimidate too many people on your way out."

I wondered if Laa might have just made a joke.

CHAPTER NINE

Kidding easily with each other, four guards accompanied me the quarter mile or so to my destination. Just outside the Arena, in a garden with vivid multi-colored flowers and walking paths laid out in the shape of fractals, a map showed a complex of buildings much larger than the Embassy. On the outer ring was a series of smaller oval arenas that gradually increased in size nearer to the center, where there were four huge Arenas. Their size suggested that each of them had more seats for spectators than any similar building on Earth. Several smallish locker rooms and practice spaces clustered in the outer rings. They grew larger, and fewer, toward the larger central Arenas.

The high arched entrance admitted us to a glittering waiting area with windows that allowed a view of the garden. The guards fell silent and rubbernecked like first-time tourists to the Vatican. Fit-looking Razors in neatly tailored sleeveless uniforms watched us enter. One of them approached and asked, "Sir?" The expression on his face would have been appropriate for a British earl addressing a Cockney chimney sweep.

I was ready to take him down a peg.

Jimmy whispered in my head. *Be respectful.*

I took a breath. "Hello. I am the Ambassador from Earth." I gestured to the guards around me. "These are my bodyguards. My assistant inquired about me coming here to give my respect to the Master. She said she was told that I could come here." I looked around. "This is truly amazing. There is nothing like it on my planet. Please excuse my ignorance. I don't want to appear disrespectful. I'm not sure if it would be better to ask to see the Master myself, I mean when he is free, of course, or if it would be better to convey my respects through the staff here."

"I can share your respects for you," said the Razor. "I'm certain he will be happy to hear indirectly." He emphasized the word "happy" in a way that implied just the opposite.

"Thank you, sir," I said through gritted teeth. "I would very much like to learn about the Arena and about dueling. I wonder if there might be someone who has time to explain the basics to me. As Laa once said to me, I know less than a larva."

"Earth Ambassador. Hmmm. Were you involved in the incident that gathered an unruly crowd close to here not long ago?"

"I was. May I say in my defense that I was more of a catalyst than an instigator."

"And is this Laa the one whose sister caused commotion within the Plix community? The one Fez took an interest in?"

"Yes, sir. You are well informed."

"So, I suppose you do need bodyguards."

"Unfortunately, I do. On the day I arrived, there was an assassination attempt that was foiled by my protection. There might have been others, if I did not travel with royal guards. One Plix challenged me to a duel. I thought I should learn more about dueling."

"While you are on the grounds of the Arena, you need not worry about being accosted. Attacks and killings here are all done within strict regulations. You may dismiss your guards, but I suppose you will need an escort when you leave. There is an area with amenities where they can wait. I know just who would be the perfect one to explain our history and laws to you in tedious detail."

He motioned to a nearby Razor, who led my guards away. He then gave me the slightest nod and led me in a different direction. I followed, trying not to gape at the splendor around me. The farther we walked, the more ordinary the surroundings became. After a hundred yards or so, he pointed to an open door, spun on his heel, and left.

I slipped into the room and discovered a thin Razor who moved without the fluidity I had seen in other aliens. He seemed older than any other alien I had seen. He regarded me for a moment before huffing. Computer terminals sat on tables. Books and files were piled haphazardly along the walls, on the floor, and on metal shelves.

"Can you pick that up?" The Razor pointed to about a ten-inch square box in a corner.

I nodded, noting he had a gleam in his eyes. I bent my knees and put my hands on opposite sides of the box. I tried to lift it, but the box felt like it was cemented to the floor. I gritted my teeth and lifted, my arms and legs straining and trembling. I managed maybe half an inch of elevation before dropping it. It landed with a thump.

Breathing hard, I told him, "Yes, I can lift it, but barely."

"You might not be a total idiot," he said. "You'd be surprised how many visitors Qaad palms off on me who assure me they can lift it before they try. And you got it off the ground. You might be worth talking to. What do you want?"

"I want to learn about duels in the Arena," I said. "I want to find out the rules about challenges. Mostly I want to learn how to get out of a challenge to duel. Can someone with razor-sharp forearms challenge a being like me without biological weapons? If challenged, what can I do to refuse?"

He sighed. "There was a time when duels were fought only between equal opponents. And only over serious matters of honor. Nowadays they fight for reputation and brag about killing others who are outmatched from the beginning. You should get respect for your prowess against equals, not disdain because you are not insectoid. Understand, I have great respect for the current Master. Our society has changed. Young Razors prowl the docks looking for aliens who know nothing about Razor Prime so they can kill and show off to their friends."

He fell silent. He looked off into the distance. I did not speak. After ten seconds or so, he focused on me again. "My name is Az. I was once Master of the Arena. Back then I would have heard your request and taken steps to ensure that any duel would be a contest of skill and courage. By strong tradition, insectoids do not challenge other species. You should be able to refuse to duel because of the biological differences between you and your challenger. But now

48

you might avoid a duel only by pleading your physical inferiority and general unworthiness to participate. I'll explain if you don't mind listening to an old Razor natter on."

"I'd appreciate it," I said. "I need all the information I can get."

"When we were sponsored into the known worlds of the universe not so very long ago, our pride in our achievements was severely shaken. Our technology was far inferior. Our science and medicine were so primitive that no beings wanted our services. Only scholars of other planets cared. They had no money. Our greatest thinkers were like the newly hatched compared to the geniuses of the universe. We became consumers of other beings' goods and services. But we could not pay for even third-class outmoded technology that was far superior to ours. It was like, how many strings of seashells would it take to buy a used steamboat? For all our individual fighting skills, there's not much demand for a knife fighter who has to face a machine gun. I love dueling, but now it's being used to prop up wounded egos. Before sponsorship royals were moving past exterminating family members of their opponents over political disputes. The lowest were gaining at least minimal respect and rights. All that is lost. We are in a dark age."

"Thank you for the explanation," I said. "I understand many things better now. My name is Liam Conner. I'm the first Earth Ambassador to make it to the Capital alive," I said. "My kind are regarded as beneath contempt by the species I meet. And I've already been challenged. I want to stay alive but I will not grovel and debase myself to save my life. My continued existence here is proof that humans are not the low lifeforms we are assumed to be. Eventually, it may be impossible to avoid dueling. If that happens, Az, I'm at least going to leave my mark on my executioner."

Az smiled. "Maybe you are the reason I have not died yet. Maybe there is still something I can contribute to Razor Prime. Let me research the history of the glorious tradition for honorable adjustments made in the past to lessen the disadvantages of beings whose physical state was not conducive to duels. Can I visit you at your embassy with what I find?"

"I would be honored to host you," I said. "The former Master of the Arena visiting would bring honor to my embassy."

He smiled and led me back to the lobby. Through the windows, I saw Qa and another Razor peering inside.

"This doesn't look good," I said to Az. I saw Qaad, the Razor I had spoken with when we entered. "Take me to where my guards are waiting." He sniffed, as if he were a chef smelling a week-old fish, and led me to a room that resembled a men's club on Earth. Az followed quietly. Two snoring guards sprawled on the floor. One was stretched out on a couch, dead to the world.

"I told them to stay sober, but they wouldn't listen," said the fourth guard, leaning unsteadily against a wall. Then she slid down the wall, blinked twice, and drifted off.

"It is such a shame that we Arena staff don't trouble ourselves with petty disagreements among outsiders," said Qaad.

"You can explain to the Master how giving intoxicants to the bodyguards of an Ambassador is a neutral action," said Az. "Ah, here he comes now."

A distinguished-looking Razor dressed in a uniform with more gold ornamentation than that of the guards strode into the room.

"Why are these bodyguards unconscious, Qaad?"

"It's just a minor event, sir. The alien's pet guards decided to indulge rather than stay sober to guard it." The Razor guide's voice had a small quaver in it as he answered.

"How did they learn about the intoxicants?" asked Az. "Did they ask for them, or did someone tell them we have drugs not available to people of their class? Was it you? Did you tell them this was a once-in-a-lifetime opportunity?"

Qaad's eyes shifted back and forth.

"I wonder how Qa found out I was here," I said. "Did you tell him?"

"What if I did? Who cares, ape-man?" asked Qaad.

"I care, as it happens," said the Master. "I will not allow visitors to be set up for an ambush."

The Master put his left hand on Qaad's shoulders, facing him. "I am disappointed in you." His right forearm flashed up. In a single swift motion, his sharp forearm ripped Qaad's stomach from his waist to just under his shoulder. Qaad's blood and organs exploded outward.

"I apologize, Conner," the Master said, stepping over the body and ignoring the blood dripping from his uniform. "Believe me, this is an outrageous betrayal of our standards. Your bodyguards will be undisturbed until they regain sobriety. I can offer you a security escort to the border of our property. Unfortunately, I cannot give you an escort to your home. That would exacerbate the Arena's violation of neutrality, which is becoming harder to sustain. As you can see."

He shook his head and glanced at the body on the floor. "We simply cannot take sides in disputes outside those that occur according to our rules and traditions. I hope you understand."

"Yes, sir," I replied. My mind was churning, searching for a way out of the mess I was in.

Az interjected, "On the other hand, Conner was kind enough to invite me to visit him before this blasphemy happened. I accept his offer and I will accompany him. If someone should happen to attack us, we will, of course, defend ourselves."

I've been trying to contact Laa, to ask her to send more guards. I can't because she is furious with someone – not you, for once. I cannot get her attention because of her heightened emotions. You can ask to stay until the guards sober up. They would let you.

I thought back at him: "And that would demonstrate to them that I am an unworthy ape-man, meritless, and beneath honor. I made a good initial impression with Az. I need him as an ally. I will have to risk leaving."

"I am grateful, Az," I said. "I would rather not fight, but if it comes to that I will do the best I can."

As we walked through the Arena grounds, I chastised myself for once again underestimating the alien environment. Az hummed and smiled. "I haven't felt so useful in quite some time. I am so happy you came today. When they attack, try to stay alive until I can help you. I would hate to have our interesting acquaintance end so soon. So few beings have the patience to listen to me for so long."

"I am a willing and grateful audience," I said.

Once we were off the Arena grounds, Qa appeared with another, smaller Razor. He looked at me and sneered. "You hid behind royal guards, behind a female Plix, and now you hide behind an old coot. Is that the best you can do?"

"So far, I haven't needed more than that to deal with you, Qa. Who's the nymph? Are you sure he can protect you?"

"He's one of my many admirers," said Qa. "He's so young he hasn't killed anybody yet so I thought I'd start him off with an easy kill – you. He'll be blooded after this. And Grandpa, if you don't interfere, I'll let you continue living."

"Excuse me, Conner," said Az. "This shouldn't take long."

Az crouched into a fighting stance in front of Qa. He didn't seem very well balanced. I had no more time to observe. The younger Razor ran at me, windmilling his short arms wildly. I got into a crouch and stayed frozen. When he got closer, I widened my eyes and opened my mouth. He ran even faster on the verge of being unable to stop. I dodged to my right at the last second. He pounded on past me unable to swerve or stop in time. I waited until he slowed and turned around. His chest was heaving and he was breathing hard. Qa said this was his first serious fight. He clearly had no idea what to do. I stayed calm, reminded myself that he wanted to kill me, and planned how to disable him with as little danger to myself as possible.

He chugged at me again, arms flailing. He was not as quick as he had been. I stood my ground. He slashed left and right, swinging both arms in long outward arcs. I feigned backing up. He swung again, one arm quickly after the other, leaving his chest unprotected. I stepped toward him, grabbing both of his extended wrists. His sharp forearms pointed outward. As long as I kept my grip, he could not kill me with his forearms. We bumped chests. He staggered back half a step.

He tugged, trying to free his arms, but he did not have the strength to break loose. I had worked for years to strengthen my hands for holding onto an opponent. With his wrists firmly in my hands, I kicked his left knee as the Taekwondo instructor taught me. He wobbled. I kicked it again. His eyes widened and he whimpered. I kicked it a third time before the knee failed. He would have fallen but I held him up off the ground. Then I kicked his right knee. Tears streamed down his face. His head swung from side to side, apparently looking for Qa. One more kick broke something in his right knee, and he faltered. He hung between my arms like a puppet with cut strings. I stepped back and let go. He fell on his face. My anger at Qa flared. He sent a totally unprepared youngster into his first fight with no supervision or support.

The Razor was out of the fight, crying and cussing. I told myself that I did not have time for sympathy. I turned to look for Az and Qa. They circled each other. Neither was bleeding. I moved stealthily toward them. Their attention was intensely focused on each other. I approached at an angle, timing my movement so that I arrived behind Qa without alerting him. I swept Qa's legs out from under him. He crashed to the ground. I kicked him in the back of his head. When he turned to look at me, Az bent and drew his forearm across Qa's exposed throat, spilling Qa's lifeblood onto the ground.

"Whew, I must be getting old," said Az. "His technique was really lousy. In the old days, he wouldn't have lasted thirty seconds. Thanks for the assist."

I felt sick to my stomach.

"Where's the other one?"

I threw up in my mouth and pointed.

"Not dead yet, eh? Do you want to kill him?'

I shook my head.

"I'll do it then."

I looked away and spat the foulness out of my mouth. Az returned a few moments later.

Az spoke as we walked. "Those were satisfying kills. Don't look so appalled. Let me explain. Nature, evolution, or whatever gods you believe in gave us weapons on our forearms and the temperament to use them. I admit we are hot-tempered and impulsive. The environment was comfortable. Food was easily available. So, we competed with each other. The strongest would gain followers, start farms, and construct homes. Then another powerful insect would challenge him or her, tear down the homes, kill the followers, and burn the crops. We were the enemies of our own civilization and progress for centuries. It kept our population down, as well as our achievements."

Az looked around before starting again. I felt relief at being alive, and anger that I had been forced into a killing game.

"Nobody knows exactly how long ago the first Master appeared. He was unbeatable. His mate was also an incredible fighter. She accumulated a large holding before they married. Those who challenged her, like those who opposed her husband, always died. When the Master destroyed a strong opponent, he would let the followers live and keep their homes intact and let the weaker ones grow crops. Followers flocked to him. Those with talent and artistic gifts lived long enough to create new concepts. Under his rule, science and medicine came into being. The Master appointed assistants who applied his rules over increasing population centers. He retired and disappeared, but his ideas lived beyond his presence."

He looked at me. I pushed down my roiling emotions and spoke. "We have figures like that in our history on Earth – powerful leaders who legends say will return to protect us in time of great need."

"We have the same mythology," said Az. "Later rulers called themselves kings or queens. They set up royal families to continue stable rule. Wise families intermarried and shared the territory they controlled. Fools fought wars and destroyed each other. We no longer breed as if our lifetimes were short. Elite families limit the number born, but we still worry about overpopulation, even though it has not been a problem for several generations. Insectoids of power developed a system of dueling that prevented wars and spared commoners. As an ape-man, you would ordinarily not have the status to respond to a challenge. However, you are an Ambassador. The royals have indicated an interest in you. A member of a prominent Plix family is indentured to you. Indirectly, you are credited with a number of deaths of the elite."

"I haven't killed anyone," I protested. "I'm just trying to stay alive."

"You talk respectfully, as if you were a peon but act like you are an equal. With their first meal, the common folk ingest the idea that their wants are secondary to those of the elite. It is obvious to us that you don't believe that. Sometimes you forget to be deferential."

So, I hadn't fooled him. Of course I hadn't. He would have died years earlier if he had accepted things at face value.

"Do all commoners think that?" I asked.

"Oh, no. There are rebels that would throw us into chaos by removing the structure that sustains our society. We treat them as threats to peace and stability. You are not a rebel. If you were, you would have been killed out of hand. However, you share some of their characteristics. Be careful not to stray too far into their dangerous way of behaving."

CHAPTER TEN

When we arrived at the embassy, the air was thick with Laa's exuded rage. She was pacing nervously, like a nuclear reactor on the verge of a meltdown.

I said, "I'd like you to meet—"

"There you are," she blurted. "I am just about ready to kill him. You have no idea how outrageous and humiliating he has been."

"Who is he?" I asked.

"As if you don't know."

"I don't. Less than an egg, remember," I said.

She finally noticed Az and stiffened.

"Don't mind me," said Az. "This sounds important."

Her head swiveled back and forth between Az and me.

"Go on," I said. "Explain before you blow a gasket."

"He is your larvae-ridden neighbor. The parasite on the body politic of Plix. I hear he doesn't even kill his own meals." She looked at me with an expression of pleading on her face that I had never seen before.

"Az, please excuse us. This is a delicate matter that I need to discuss with Laa in private."

"It was just getting interesting," he protested, smiling.

Laa and I went into a small room. She moved her mouth as if tasting something spoiled before she spoke.

"Thank you. That was embarrassing. Gi has been regaling me with intimate details of his plans to rape me."

I raised my eyebrows.

"As I said before, I will not sell your favors. I understand I lack the cultural background to understand how terrible that is, but even on my planet, such talk would be extremely unseemly and upsetting. I hope it is clear that I will never, never cooperate with his plans."

"I didn't think you would. Not really."

"At the risk of offending you even more, can I ask how is that possible?" I asked. "Gi moves like a slug and looks as athletic as a snail. Surely you can slice him into tiny chunks without breathing hard."

She studied my face for a moment. "I keep forgetting how naïve and alien you are." She sighed. "Gi would never face me alone. He is too much of a coward. He keeps a group of ten very pretty male Plix around. When they tire of playing with each other's privates, they look for a female to humiliate and debase."

I blanched. "I had no idea."

Laa reached out and touched my arm.

"I believe you. Let's greet your guest."

Az was speaking to Ef when we returned. She spotted me and fled.

"I recognize you," said Laa to Az. "You were the Arena Master for decades."

He smiled. "I was."

"Oh, Conner, you should have seen him in battle. He was an artist. Never a wasted movement. Never a loss of concentration. As Master, he fought to represent the royals, so every match was significant. No petty revenge for insults or imagined slights."

"You are too kind," said Az.

"And he had the grace and wisdom to retire while at the very peak of his skills. He was unwilling to perform at less than the best of his artform."

"Now that really is much too kind," said Az. "I performed all the way through my prime. It was clear to me that I would be soon challenged by younger, fitter Razors who had better skills than what few remained with me. I'm gratified to hear that my diminished abilities were not clearly obvious. I was too proud of my reputation to die a shadow of my former self in the Arena. Retiring was an act of vanity that I sometimes question in my dotage."

"You are legendary, sir. You had such amazing technique that I have no doubt that you would still be a formidable opponent today."

"Not true," said Az. "We were attacked by two Razors earlier today. Conner put them both down." He nodded at me.

"Really? He killed them?" asked Laa.

"No," I said. "I defended myself, but I did not kill them."

"He's not an insectoid," said Az. "He's a likable barbarian but he is not one of us. I didn't see his first fight clearly, but apparently, he got inside the guard of the Razor and smashed both his knees. With Qa, he kicked Qa's legs out from under him from behind. He's got timing, balance, and guts. He spotted their weaknesses and took advantage of them."

"I would not have believed it if someone else had told me," said Laa. "I'm sorry I did not see it for myself."

"I don't want to kill, or to die for that matter," I said. "I don't know anything about duels, but neither maneuver would be possible in a confined space or with a knowledgeable opponent. I want to learn how to avoid fighting."

"He's clueless, Az," she said. "But think what a duelist he would be if he was able to compete on the same level as insectoids. I remember One Leg from my youth, who won five duels on a prosthetic leg below his knee. When the legendary One Arm was allowed to wear a shield on the stump of his elbow from a birth defect, he lived through a dozen contests."

"I remember," said Az. "I plan to review Arena records for other times when steps were taken to make contests fair by allowing adjustments for particular individuals. We've never had an ape-man contend against an insectoid, but duels used to be limited to only Razors. Recently ape-men have been allowed to match each other in preliminary events. I think I can persuade the Master to make allowances for Conner."

"I. Don't. Want. To. Duel," I said. "Did I fail to mention that? I asked you two to help me avoid killing or being killed."

"As you told me, avoiding a duel might not be possible in the long run," said Az. "I'm certain you are not a coward. You are the sole member of your species on a planet teeming with physically dangerous beings who have more natural weapons than you do, but you don't hide in a burrow. You had the option of asking for sanctuary until your guards recovered. I didn't suggest it because that would have been extremely insulting."

"I did not set out with the intention of battling to the death," I said. "If we had not been attacked, I would not have gotten involved in bloodletting. I might have stayed in the Arena, but I admit I do not react well to being threatened. I never have. It's a character flaw of mine." I sighed. "We'd be honored, Az, if you would stay for dinner. We are still getting organized, so I can't promise you much."

"Oh, no, my wife would be displeased if I didn't arrive home on time."

"Perhaps some other time then, when she might join us," I said.

"I'll tell her about today. She'll be interested, I'm sure." He turned to go, and then stopped and turned back. "Definitely, the best way for you to learn about duels is for you to see them. The Arena has duels scheduled for the next couple of years, and reservations are already sold out. I have to warn you that a human walking around would draw unwanted attention. Ticket holders would be likely to kill any non-insectoid they happened upon as part of the festivities without even thinking about it. I suggest you wait. After we fulfill those engagements, we could be more flexible. You could view practices and speak with some apes who spar with young insectoids as part of the insectoids' preparation for contesting with more dangerous opponents."

"Thank you again for all your help," I said.

...

The four guards who stayed overnight in the Arena arrived quietly about noon the next day. They blinked as if the sunlight was painful, and they moved stiffly and jumped at sudden noises. I immediately called the rest of the guards together. The rest of the force assembled in ranks facing them, as I had planned.

"Welcome home," I told them. "Why don't you explain to your brothers and sisters in arms why you did not make it home yesterday? Who'd like to start?"

The four looked at the ground, the sky, and each other. None spoke. The other guards looked on impassively.

"Make yourselves comfortable," I said. When the four moved to sit, I said, "Not you four. It's noon and hot. Everyone else has been fulfilling their duties so they can sit down. You have not. We are waiting for your explanation. You can stand until you give it."

The four wobbled and looked confused. Finally, one of them mumbled an apology.

"I can barely hear that. Repeat what you said," I said.

She spoke louder and apologized more coherently, admitting she had been intoxicated.

"Good," I said. She moved to sit down.

"Wait, did I tell you to sit? The four of you were involved in the escapade as a group. We're all waiting for the rest of you to speak."

She remained standing. After a moment, another mumbled through the story. And then another. By the time the fourth one finished, they were all struggling to remain erect.

"You may sit."

They collapsed. "You will see the doctor and, after that, you will be confined to your quarters until further notice. When the doctor tells me you are fit for duty, you will come to me individually and tell me why this will never happen again. Dismissed."

I approached one of the guards I had seen talking with Hy. "Contact Hy and invite him to stop by when it is convenient for him. He'll be able to see you, and if there's a particular prey or drink he likes, let me know. I will provide it."

I needed to talk to Doc, but she would be attending to the four guards. I needed to talk to Hy, but there was no way to know when he might come around. Restless and uncertain, feeling uneasy in my skin, I decided to talk to Laa. I had questions. She would have answers. Some answers, anyway. I went looking for her.

As usual, she was at the center of activity.

"Do you have some free time?" I asked her.

"I'm in the middle of something."

"Can it be delayed?" I asked. "I'd like to walk around the neighborhood and talk with you."

"You're asking me," she said. "You're not telling me, so yes. I will walk with you. Should we take security with us?"

"I don't think we need to," I said. "At the moment I don't think anybody is plotting to kill me."

CHAPTER ELEVEN

We walked around the neighborhood. I asked about the little village of one-room shops and shacks that surrounded the Embassy. She had already met the residents and introduced them to me. Some people sold food from their homes. Others sewed, did rough carpentry, or sold good-luck charms. A few told fortunes and made love potions and various enchanted items to break hexes. None admitted to selling curses, but I suspected that was an important part of their businesses. Why else was there traffic in spell-breaking? All were curious about the alien who they'd heard about and were grateful that the neighborhood was calmer than it had been before my arrival. When I asked one weaver what I might do to help, he said, "The problem is getting the capital to expand. If I could borrow money to buy another loom, I'm certain I would pay it off quickly, but the bank won't back fledgling businesses like mine, so I cannot take orders beyond my capacity to fill them. I'm stuck with just making enough to feed me and my family after taxes. Gangs raid businesses that have a little success, so everybody like me is trapped at the bottom of the swamp."

Others told similar stories: Inadequate buildings, raids from gangs, and the lack of ability to transport goods were limitations.

"I have to keep the guards occupied, and training is not enough," I said to Laa. "I worked in construction for years back on Earth before I saved enough to start a business of my own. What if I put them to work on building shops and houses? I can work along with them."

"It would encourage cooperation," said Laa. "I can talk to the bank about making small loans from your deposited funds. The bank would have no risk and it'd collect a management fee. The neighbors would be grateful, and it would help with your security."

"Do it," I said. We continued our walk. "It looks different, doesn't it, Laa?"

"What looks different?" she asked.

"The world. How things are done. What normal means," I said. "As a person with unquestioned privilege, it all seems so natural that you don't even think about it. The same society seen from the point of view of those lacking advantages seems arbitrary and unfair. I wonder if you would have gotten acquainted with the residents in the same way if you'd been acting in your former position."

"Maybe not," she said.

"When you were a person of status, you acted ethically," I said. "You protected your family, unlike your sister. You sacrificed that status, not knowing what would happen. If that entailed setting up a couple of murders, it made sense from where you were."

"Your position is different," said Laa.

"Yes," I said. "I've never been a person of power. Here, I have no family to protect. I have no one protecting me. My threats served my interest alone. I'm not proud of that, but it seemed necessary. Threats and fear are not great motivators. I hope you and the guards gain enough from being associated with me that our mutual interests will protect each other."

"You had the chance to sell my sexual services," said Laa.

"I might have rented them out," I said. "I would have retained ownership and rented them more than once if the market allowed. However, I have ethical standards of my own. And besides, I wouldn't sleep well with you in the embassy dreaming up revenge."

"You are a wise alien," said Laa.

We continued to walk.

"I don't understand the necklace thing," I said to Laa. "Is the necklace a form of money? Will it become plainer if I buy things?"

"No. It is an old tradition. I suppose in the distant past it was a string of beads. You'd probably pop one off to buy a meal or clothing. Now it reflects wealth symbolically for the elite. Some of the lowest in society leave their necklaces with merchants like a promissory note until the rent or whatever is paid. Then they retrieve the necklace. There is an invisible complex system monitoring financial transactions. You can buy a table or a meal without anything physically changing hands. The system makes adjustments automatically."

"I think we should order similar outfits for all the guards so we recognize one another in a fight," I said. "Maybe the weavers nearby can make them. We can split up the order to involve all the local weavers."

"I agree," she said.

"A few of the gang members are females," I said. "Do females fight duels? Do they fight against males?"

"Yes, and yes, although we are not as obsessed with honor as males in general. There have been Arena Mistresses from time to time. I think the original Master got a lot of ideas from his wife. She was a legendary warrior and owned a huge piece of land before they got together."

"That makes sense," I said. "Az mentioned her. I imagine Gi never made overtures to you before you became indentured."

"Back when I was a free personage, he wouldn't have dared. I would have called him out for a duel. He can only entrap females who are very poor or very naïve. Is that the case on Earth?"

"Sadly, it is," I said. "I believe we can puncture his overgrown pride and drain his monetary resources at the same time. We should be able to leave him uncertain about whether or not he's been fleeced."

"I'm interested," she said. "Tell me more."

...

"How are the guards, Doc?" I asked, entering her office alone.

"Dehydrated, undernourished, and still showing traces of the intoxicant in their blood and fat cells. It will take time to exit their bodies. It did not help that you delayed their getting treatment and forced them to remain standing."

"I'm sure you're angry with me," I said. "You are justified in those feelings. I might have sent them to you when they arrived and

I did not." I put my hand out palm first so she would not interrupt. "I have no doubt they were enticed, tempted, and essentially poisoned. They were taken from the streets and shown a world they didn't even know existed. If they were children like Cub Scouts or Brownies on my world and I was the den leader, I would have been sympathetic, but—"

"You're going to say, 'but they were not children,'" said Doc. "They were hired to protect you. They failed in their most important duty. As leader of the guards, you had to take action or lose the respect of your entire security force. I understand all that. I understand that others in your situation would have executed them on the spot."

"So, you're not angry?" I asked.

"I used to be angry, frustrated, discouraged ¬– take your pick. Before this," said Doc. "Now I feel a twinge of hope because of you."

I must have looked confused. I certainly felt that way.

"You might have guessed I was not born on this planet," said Doc. "I'm here to help them develop."

"Are you – your species, I mean – are you sponsoring the Razors?" I asked.

"Exactly. They are amazingly bright and creative. After the first Master and Mistress changed the rules, the sciences, medicine, and art flourished. They went from savage to semi-civilized in a few generations. It was like when Hammurabi's Code was published on Earth. The 'eye for an eye' declaration, which sounds barbaric to us now, was a great ethical leap forward. It replaced the idea of death for an eye with an attempt to provide punishment equivalent to the crime."

"Improved, yes, but Az said your sponsorship ended up making them feel inadequate and they regressed to more killing very quickly here."

"Very true," said Doc. "Unfortunately, natives of newly sponsored worlds often become intimidated by others in the universe. Razors regressed toward indiscriminate killing. But you are not like that. Razors like Az and Fez don't understand your reluctance to kill. You are the only human on the planet. They aren't used to thinking of individuals as important. A healthy sense of confusion comes before change."

I groaned. "As if I didn't have enough to worry about before. Hey, your species can sponsor Earth."

"We sponsor Razor Prime. They sponsor Earth," she said. "Finding out your people are a tiny part of a much more sophisticated social universe is a major shock. Why do you think people on Earth would deal with it better than the Razors did?"

"Maybe we wouldn't," I said, thinking about humans' reckless waste of limited resources, the disparity between rich and poor, and our reluctance to take responsibility for our actions. "If we aren't ready yet, so be it. But the Razors became sponsors by accident because they didn't recognize a cell phone. They weren't ready to sponsor another people."

"No, but they became the sponsor anyway," she said.

I folded my hands together and leaned toward her. "Sometimes on Earth a three-year-old child will want a puppy or kitten as a pet. A wise parent will refuse. But, if, say, a well-meaning grandparent gave the child a pet, parents would supervise closely and give the pet away if the child mistreated it, regardless of whether or not the child threw a tantrum."

Doc looked away from me.

I spoke louder, irritated by her behavior. "You can take the Earth away from the immature Razors. The Razors are not ready to sponsor my people."

Doc turned her back to me. I felt my face get hot as my anger flared.

"Talk to me," I demanded.

Not turning, Doc's skin took on the pale green color of the room. She spoke so softly I could barely make out the words. "We have an obligation to the Razors. Some of them have started to question their knee-jerk response to all problems by killing. Historically, they controlled over-population by mass killings. Even though it is no longer a problem, the old ways die hard. Elite families that feel threatened can have more offspring than allowed. Then the authorities try to keep things in balance by killing part of the family. That reinforces the old thought process. Elite Razors now foster out most of their offspring. The ones the families keep are nurtured and educated, which means families consider individuals valuable. They are starting to increase their concern for others."

She spoke louder.

"Sponsoring has forced them, at least some of them, to face ethical issues they weren't even aware of. Removing their sponsorship would interfere with the chance for emotional and ethical advancement. They already consider themselves inadequate. Taking their sponsoring away would set them back for who knows how long."

I was distracted by a throbbing vein in my temple. As I spoke, I realized my voice was too loud. "I can understand why the Razors kill so easily. But what is there in the development of your species that gives you an excuse to aid and abet murder? Why don't you care that they torment and torture humans along their developmental path? How is it that your species determined humans are totally worthless?"

She turned to face me again. Her skin became as smooth as the paint on the walls. "We haven't," she said.

I shook as my anger grew. "But your species decided that whatever happens to us is irrelevant. Have you, infallible gods that you are, achieved such moral perfection that your judgments cannot be questioned by lesser beings like me? Is that it, goddess? Should this pathetic worm grovel before you?"

She blinked several times. "We are aware of our ethical failure regarding humans. Our policy is very controversial. We are not at all certain what we chose is moral. I admit the relatively small number of murdered humans lets us avoid thinking about it. My superiors have decided that we have committed to helping Razors. We are not committed to humans. I don't agree with my superiors, but I am bound by their decision. If you like, I will leave. You never see me again."

"Hell, no!" I said, spit flying from my mouth. "You're not going to get off the hook so easily. If your people want to use me for your divine purpose, I insist you remain in the Embassy and provide medical services to whoever needs it whenever they need it. I want you to sit in on meetings, patch my wounds, and keep me alive until they slaughter me in front of your eyes. I wish I could force all your people to witness it first-hand. I can't, but, by God, I demand it of you."

I struggled for breath and then continued, "I will not kill sentient beings. But tell your holier-than-me people that if you leave, I will dig a pit. I will crawl into it and never come out of it until the Razors come to butcher me. When they come for me, I will snivel and beg. They will consider me a coward. I will lose any influence I have with them. The Razors will conclude that I am the unworthy piece of shit your people consider me. That will undo whatever plans you have for using my life as a way to further their development. It will reinforce their sense of superiority. And, of course, it will reinforce your goddamned moral supremacy, too."

Her skin flashed alternating patterns of red and blue circles.

"Razors splash blood on themselves out of fear and ignorance, holding onto behavior that once had a purpose. Your species knowingly swims in the blood of innocents and tries to justify it with noble-sounding excuses. Are you mature enough to sponsor another species?"

I slammed the door as I left the office.

CHAPTER TWELVE

It wasn't long after that I had the misfortune of seeing the insect guards eat. They sat at tables with long benches and pounded their fists on the tables in anticipation. When the noise reached the level of a departing jet plane, a parade of hunters carrying cages entered the room. Squirming bugs smashed against the walls of the cages as if trying to flee. On command the hunters lifted the cage door. The bugs poured out and scattered.

Guards fought each other as they stalked the bugs. When a guard snatched a bug, he or she bit the living creature. The unfortunate victim screamed, and blood and bodily fluids spurted from its wounds. Often a bug was ripped away from one guard by another one. The sounds in the room were horrendous.

The bugs were not defenseless. They used their claws and teeth, if they had them, but they were clearly outmatched. The meal continued until all of the bugs were dead and devoured. Then, among the body parts and gore, the guards belted out songs about past battles and sexual conquests. The tunes resembled Asian music.

Jimmy reminded me of an Irish song I had learned. In a rare moment of silence, I began, "Come out ye Black and Tans. Come and fight me like a man." The guards fell silent. I followed that song with "The Rising of the Moon." My finale was "Finnegan's Wake." The guards hooted and stomped their feet during the chorus.

Even though I hadn't engaged in the mayhem, my performance apparently helped establish me as a leader who could be trusted.

...

It turned out that Hy was fond of a rare type of insect, and the hunter had captured a mating pair of them. Naturally, my dietary needs were significantly different enough from everyone else's. Hy brought a few friends with him. After the meal, we met alone.

"I had a chance to talk with my relatives earlier," he said. "They think you're weird, but they like you. They wonder what you are going to do with the guards confined to their quarters."

"That's where I need your advice," I said. "So far, I've been lucky. The guards are good youngsters really. Even as gang members, they did a good deal of protection for the residents. Their families live in the neighborhood, and they looked after young ones in the streets whose families deserted them. They showed loyalty to each other, and it appears that they want to belong to something bigger than themselves. They jumped at the chance to become guards with a steady income and a purpose they can be proud of. But I need to discipline the four without losing their respect. I don't know how to do that. I don't want to just execute them."

"They're not royal guards," said Hy. "We have so many aimless youngsters waiting to join us that executing a few for lapses just enhances our reputation. Surely there must be hard filthy labor that needs to be done, like cleaning out the sewers or rebuilding roads. Set them to work to accomplish a task like that until it is finished. Then let them rejoin the others. You ought to have the others laboring on projects, too, as well as practicing fighting. Construction work is a good idea. It will keep them in shape and tired at the end of the day. When you work with them as hard as they do, you earn their respect."

"That's the sort of information I need," I said. "I don't need officers. I need people who work for a living, Sergeants like you. If you know any retired leaders or the like, send them my direction, will you?"

"I know somebody," said Hy. "Dob is her name. She's prickly, hard to get along with, but she might be interested. I wondered if you might offer her a job. I brought her along."

70

"I'd like to meet her. Please ask her to join us."

Hy stepped out for a moment. Soon he was back with a Razor beside him. The Razor looked around the room and sniffed. She was bigger than Hy. The sleeve on her right wrist was rolled up to prominently show the stub where, presumably, her hand used to be.

"I ain't interested in no charity job," Dob said. "This bugger seems to think he ought to help me since it was saving his ass that caused me to lose my hand."

"Do you mind telling me how that happened?" I asked.

"I stuck it out too far toward a goddamn rebel who chopped it off," she said.

"Then she stuck the stump in his face," said Hy. "The blood streaming out blinded him long enough for her to open his stomach up like a ripe melon."

"Yeah, like I was going to let the bastard away with that," she said. "The royal guards decided they didn't want no cripple in their ranks. What about you?" She leaned toward me and snarled. "I was born from two common Razors. Nobody gave me nothing I didn't earn. I don't take charity. Why do you want a cripple?"

"I don't have any jobs for cripples or anybody else who can't do what is required. Can you fight?"

"Yeah."

"Can you teach others how to fight – without killing the slow and lazy ones?" I asked.

"That makes it harder, but I suppose I can," answered Dob.

"Then, as far as I can tell, you aren't crippled," I said. "Back on my planet centuries ago we had warriors called Vikings. The wildest of them were Berserkers. When they got a hand chopped off, they did exactly what you did and called it 'whale spouting.'"

I paused. "I was born to the most common of common people on Earth. Everything I got I earned from people who didn't think a dark-skinned hick from a farm would be able to do it so I understand you had to be better than everyone else before they gave you credit for being as good as the next one. I absolutely know whoever kicked you out of the royal guards is a royal idiot. When can you start?"

...

Dob terrified the guards, and they loved her. Not long after she started, she sent word to me that she needed me to talk to the primate guards about fighting insectoids. When I arrived at the training grounds, I found all the trainees lined up around the field, jabbering and joking, looking as if they were waiting for a rock concert to start.

"Rumor has it," Dob said to me, "that you took on and defeated a Razor one on one. I thought perhaps you might share some tactics with us. Maybe do a walkthrough."

I could tell she had something more in mind, but I thought it might be interesting.

"Sure," I said. "Affe, Singe, join me."

The two simians came to me. "Dob, if you would, select an insectoid for a demonstration."

"How about me?" she asked. She slipped metal tubes over her forearms, covering the sharp biological blades, and took a ready position.

"Okay, we apes have no defense against her slashes. We have to stay out of her reach. The best way to do that is to work as a team. Four would be optimal. We form a square. When she approaches one of us, he runs and the others retain the shape."

The three of us took positions around Dob. She feinted at Affe and ran toward me. I ran away, calling for the other two to keep the shape. When she swung toward Singe, he bolted without looking back. I couldn't blame him, but he ran so fast Affe and I couldn't keep up. Dob turned.

"Singe, you went too far too fast," I said. "I know it's scary, but you have to support the team. Remember, if she kills the two of us, you won't have a prayer of surviving. Affe and I can try to go front and back, but it's much more effective if there are three of us. We want to frustrate the attacker, keep her moving, and wear her down. She gets tired. We can take turns. The three of us combined have more endurance than one of her."

"You won't always be able to team up," said Dob. "What about when you are isolated?"

"Pray and look for a partner," I said.

"And when that fails?" she asked, coming at me.

"Most kills come quickly for insectoids," I said, backing away.

"The idea is the same: dodge, avoid, and use your endurance."

Dob and I circled each other. I yielded ground after every assault. I let her approach close enough to swing but stayed just out of range. "Every missing swing uses up energy," I said. I maneuvered over the torn-up surface of the field and spun near a hole torn in the turf. Dob lost her balance momentarily.

"A less experienced fighter might have fallen or been distracted," I said. "That might have given me enough advantage to make an attack."

"Well done," said Dob. "A less experienced fighter might have tripped himself or allowed me to come close enough to strike over the uneven ground."

She stalked me like a cat after a mouse for some time. I wondered if she was ever going to tire. I was sweating and breathing hard. She had to be running out of energy, but I sure couldn't tell it. "I'd hope by now my buddies would be able to help me, but a battle continues until it is over." She swiped. I jumped back. I wobbled on my feet. Dob pushed forward eagerly. She swung her right arm. I ducked under it, slid past, and punched the back of her knee with my fist as I passed. She clouted me across the chest as she fell.

I put up my hands. "I'm dead. That would have opened my chest and killed me." I offered her a hand to help up.

The guards cheered.

"You had the chance to kick the back of my knee and put me on the ground," she said quietly. With the noise of the trainees she was not audible to them.

"Not without the risk of injuring you seriously," I said softly. "Even one kick might have broken your leg or shattered your kneecap if it struck at the wrong angle. I didn't want to do that. Who would replace you while you healed?"

"You'd keep me on if I was injured?" she asked.

"I hope I'm not as dumb as the royals," I answered.

"Listen up," announced Dob. "I declare that exercise a draw. Conner had a chance to kill me before he bled out. He got me to the ground, which was his aim. I was lucky that my flailing arm caught him. If you learn nothing else from the demonstration, remember what Conner said, 'Never give up. Never give in.'"

Two days later I heard a guard sing a song about the contest. The movements were cleverly compared to a sexual seduction.

Jimmy reminded me that I had studied *Beowulf.* I shared with the guards a bit of what I remembered. The troops were impressed by my recitation.

CHAPTER THIRTEEN

Over time, Laa and I were able to establish peace and stability in an ever-expanding circle around the embassy. The ranks of the guards were raised to patrol the increasing area. We hired members from many species and arbitrated the quarrels between them. In two years, shanties became cottages that became houses. The neighborhood became one of the few where all species were tolerated at worst and welcomed at best. Businesses operating on shoestrings developed into established enterprises. The competition was fierce, but we kept it bloodless and those with similar skills gradually recognized the advantages of cooperation. The royals contracted with us for peacekeeping so they could deploy their forces to control increasing disorder and rebellion elsewhere.

Doc gave me supplements that, combined with construction labor and practice with Dob and Hy, made me faster, stronger, and more agile than I had been at my peak. Demonstrations between Dob and me turned into major entertainment events.

Laa brought me to an artists' cooperative in a rambling dwelling they bought at a substantial discount although they did not know about the reduced price. The first room's floor had an irregular surface like cobblestones. It wobbled as we walked on it. One room had a negative pressure entrance to keep an odor inside that made me gag. Another room flashed lights and would have caused seizures to people with epilepsy. The only exhibit I enjoyed was a tactile maze.

Az visited the embassy regularly with his much younger wife, who enjoyed the visits as much as he did. Gi dropped in without invitation frequently to enjoy meals and ogle Laa. She ignored him, which only made him more interested. Finally, perhaps deciding I was nearly socially acceptable, he invited me over. I accepted and asked Laa to join me. I had stopped giving her commands quite some time earlier. "Have you been to the Plix Embassy frequently?" I asked her.

"Hardly ever. I was employed by the royals, not by my planet. I lived and worked in another section of the Capital."

Gi smiled and waved as we approached.

"Thanks for coming. I don't believe you've seen my personal bodyguards before. Aren't they decorative?"

Tall, fit-looking Plix males marched out of the embassy two by two. They were dressed in silky sleeveless tunics embroidered with gold and scarlet threads. Ten in all, they formed a line on one side of the entrance. Ten other servants in a variety of less spectacular clothing formed on the other side.

"Thanks for inviting me," I said. "They are indeed impressive. I hope you don't mind that I brought Laa with me. She told me she has only been here rarely and I thought this would be a good opportunity for her."

He rubbed his hands together. "She enhances this place with her beauty." He gave her a look that back on Earth was best described as leering.

He then led us on a tour of the extensive building. Laa alternated between keeping her eyes demurely averted from Gi's face and giving him intense but brief eye contact. Each time she looked at him, Gi nearly jumped out of his skin. After the tour, he took us into a formal garden where shaded tables and chairs formed the shape of an oval.

"Laa, go look at the flowers," I commanded. "Gi and I have important male things to discuss."

She rose gracefully and sashayed away.

Gi leaned toward me. "Have you thought about my offer? My research proved that you can extend your privileges over Laa to other males."

"Gi, I hope you don't think I have been stringing you along," I said. Although, of course, I had been. "I now believe you are correct about that. However, this is a brand-new situation for me. Laa is a valuable possession. I don't want her damaged. In a perverse way, I actually sort of like her. Gossips tell me – not that I believe them – that your preferences include a level of aggression that might harm her."

"That is so untrue."

"Good. So, you can assure me no more restraint or physicality than is needed would be involved?"

"Of course."

"Good, good. And you can assure me that there would be no discrepancy in number? Nothing more than you and her?"

"Absolutely," Gi answered.

His skill at lying was impressive. It showed how important practice is for all skills.

"Excellent," I said. "I accept your word." For the tons of hogwash it was worth I added in a thought for Jimmy's enjoyment.

"So, perhaps today we can consummate the event?" Gi asked.

I laughed. "Now, Gi, you have promised me a fair return for the sharing. But we have not negotiated the amount. I would be foolish to give away a prize before knowing the price. To add a little spice to the adventure, I'll let Laa negotiate the price for your interaction. Once the price is agreed upon, we can set the schedule. I think the surprise will enhance the event, don't you?"

"Yes, of course."

On the way back Laa confirmed that she overheard every word. "You told me he's taken money for himself that should belong to your planet," I said. "I'll split the price fifty-fifty with your family."

"You don't need to encourage me," Laa said.

"I know," I said. "But I enjoy rebalancing the scales of life away from exploitation when I have a chance. It's another character flaw of mine."

...

The next morning Laa spoke to me.

"I have extracted every possible penny from Gi. We can reel him

77

in whenever we want."

"Okay, please contact him, but let's leave the exact time today uncertain and have him sweat for a few hours first."

When everything was ready, I sent for Gi. He was highly excited when he came through the door. My guards stopped the Plix he brought with him, informing them there had been recent threats and asked for identification from each one. I grabbed Gi by his elbow and hustled him down the hall. He didn't look back. I led him upstairs and down, left and right, moving rapidly. Gi moved as if hypnotized. When he slowed, he blinked and swung his head back and forth.

"She's ready," I said. "Believe me, this is going to be a real surprise. I isolated the whole wing of the embassy and told my staff no matter what they hear not to interfere."

"And my men?" asked Gi, frowning.

"Don't worry," I said. "This place is a maze with all the construction going on. They'll never be able to find the right room and disturb the two of you. She's right through that door."

Gi hesitated.

"Is she drugged?" he asked.

"Drugged?" I laughed. "I don't think Laa uses drugs. This has been a tough day for her so she might be a bit on edge. I promise I will leave you entirely alone with her. Remember, you promised not to be too harsh with her." I patted his shoulder. "Go to it."

I slipped around the corner and stopped. After about twenty seconds, I heard Laa say loudly and sharply, "You? What the hell do you want?" Then I heard the door close, and after that I heard a soft sob. Jimmy gleefully informed me it came from Gi. I tiptoed away and returned fifteen minutes later.

"Well, how was it?" I asked Gi, who was sitting on a stair step leading to the next higher level. The expression on his face was like that of a child who just learned that Christmas was canceled this year.

"Uh, you know how discreet I am," said Gi. I did indeed. He had regaled me with his sexual exploits with boring regularity.

"And I know Laa will never ever say a word about what happened."

"Really?" he asked, perking up.

"Oh, yes. She'll pretend you were never here. This will be just

78

between you and her. I advise you not to brag too much, though. I won't do this for anybody else, but you deserved it. I don't want to be swamped with offers."

"I think you're right," said Gi, smiling. "Let's keep it private."

"And if you don't mind—" I pulled my necklace from my collar but left it around my neck.

Gi looked at me and hesitated. I tilted my head and raised my eyebrows with all of the mock innocence I could muster. Luckily, Gi had never bothered to learn how to read my emotion or apparently the emotions of anyone else he judged to be unimportant.

He took out his payment mechanism and touched the necklace. I stuffed it back into my shirt collar without a glance. I felt it move against my neck and cheek. After I escorted him out of the building, I looked at my chain, it had morphed into a smooth platinum rope. The pendant had morphed to white gold etched with an intricate design of roses. The gem changed to a brilliant emerald the size of a quarter.

Laa looked at it and commented, "Very chic. A royal would show it off with pride. I decided it would be suspicious if my family suddenly started spending money like it was going out of style. Gi might get wind of it and wonder. So, I took my share of the profits and locked them into a trust for the next twenty years."

...

When Az finally contacted me to inform me that apes would be practicing and possibly sparring with insectoids at the Arena, I arranged with Singe and Affe to attend to watch how other apes fought. Expecting to be anonymous, I put on the patched clothing I had worn when I left the spaceship. The three of us joined a flowing river of apes and other species going to the Arena. Some wore good clothes. Others were dressed in little more than rags. Doc accompanied us, lugging a bag of medical supplies I hoped we weren't going to need. "Be sure to convey my greeting to the sadists back home, Doc," I told her. "I hope the entertainment will be gory enough to please them."

We shuffled through the doors and headed toward one of the

many outer rings. The ring itself consisted of a padded mat with a series of concentric ovals marked on it. The inner ring was about ten meters across in the shorter dimension and twenty across in the larger dimension. Two larger rings doubled in size of the inner oval. We watched a number of ape-on-ape matches, looking for wrestling moves we didn't know, and making mental notes about which contestants might make good guards. The atmosphere of the crowd was happy. Local favorites got cheers, and applause followed each match for both contestants. Then a female Plix came to the ring.

"Well, well, you apes fight well for inferior creatures," she shouted. "I hope you enjoy tonight because I'm going to do everything I can to put an end to this desecration of the Arena. I will award twelve ounces of pure gold to any ape who can last ten minutes in the ring with me."

The crowd booed and jeered.

"Okay, if that is too hard for you, I will lock a metal sleeve around the length of my left forearm. Ten minutes. You are used to running away from predators, hiding in trees, and crawling into caves. Surely, someone here should be foolish or desperate enough to take my offer."

A being slipped up beside me and looked at me intently. He looked sort of familiar.

"Is that really you?" he asked.

Hearing his voice gave me the clue I needed. He was thinner and shaggier than when I last saw him. He looked from side to side and seemed unable to sit still.

"You drove the hovercraft from the port," I said.

"Yeah, and I must have been insane to mess with that Plix bitch," he said. "They threw me in prison and then they let me go. I guess they wanted to toy with me before putting me out of my misery. Razors don't bother me, but Plix have been searching for me ever since. I didn't dare return to my job as a driver. My friends tell me strange Plix ask where I am. They offer rewards for my location."

"Listen, I can help you. I have a place where you'd be safe."

"Oh no, I've heard these lies before. You must have done a deal with the Plix to survive. I won't let you betray me. If I had enough gold, I would disappear into the countryside where they'd never find me."

He jumped out of his seat and ran to the ring before I had the chance to explain.

"I'll take your money, bitch," he said to the Plix.

"Hop on in, dead ape. The time starts now."

The driver ran to the inner edge of the outermost oval. "Come and get me."

"No, you coward. Come to the inner ring."

"What? Are you too decrepit to run all the way out here? I'll make it easier for you. I'll stay inside the middle ring."

The crowd started yelling insults and catcalls at the Plix. With a scowl on her face, she advanced to the middle ring and began to stalk her prey. The driver dodged and danced, avoiding the Plix. She tried to cut off his space, but she was half a step slow. She sliced his skin twice, but not deeply. A timekeeper called out the passing time at thirty second intervals until the last thirty seconds. Then he began to count out each second.

Bleeding and sweating, the driver began to dance just out of the Plix's reach. When the announcer said, "Over," the driver whooped. He bowed to the crowd and then to the Plix. As he stood erect, the Plix stepped up to him and slit open his stomach. Blood spurted and his body collapsed. His eyes showed more surprise than pain as he lay on the mat trying to push his exposed organs back inside his body. His mouth opened but he made no sound. He spasmed and then became motionless.

"Oops," she said. "Time expired. My mistake. Will somebody come clean up this mess? And somebody tell Conner he can expect the same."

I felt rage boil up inside. Although Singe and Affe grabbed my arms, I tore free immediately. I rose from my seat.

"You can tell me yourself," I said. "I'm here. Just who are you speaking for when you threaten me?"

"Why don't you come on up and ask me personally?" she said. "Maybe you can make me tell you."

"Maybe I can," I said. Ignoring Doc's pleas, I stepped into the ring.

CHAPTER FOURTEEN

The Plix smiled and gestured for me to come to her. I shook my head and motioned for her to come to me. She strutted around the ring. I felt my mind grow calm. I pushed away my roiling anger and planned my moves with more care than I had in my jujutsu matches. My life was on the line. I ran at her and turned as if suddenly aware of my vulnerability. She laughed out loud. She tucked her right elbow into her side and swiped in a narrow arc. I stepped closer but she continued her shortened slash.

It was obvious that she was avoiding making a longer strike that would allow me to step inside and reach her body as I had done in earlier fights with insectoids. Someone had scouted my fighting style. There was no other reason for her to give up so much of her offense. It wasn't a good adaptation, but it also limited my offense. The realization made me more determined than ever to question the killer. Had one of my people been spying on me? I circled. She followed.

I moved to her left. She swung her left arm out. I let her hit me with the metal sleeve and delivered a kick to her midsection in response. Her attention focused on my in-and-out movements. I moved, drawing her close to the driver's body. She stepped in the driver's pooled blood, slipped, and fell on her face. I jumped on her back, twisting her right arm into an armbar with the sharp outside forearm facing down. The edge cut into her back. She extended her left arm but that was a useless move. In a wrestling match, I would have gone for a double chicken wing and then flipped her to her back and pinned her. But this was decidedly not wrestling. I positioned my body to hold her so her face was down toward the mat.

"You're as tricky as they said you'd be," she said. "It won't do you any good. I won't talk. You can kill me, but I won't tell you a thing."

"You elite insectoids are into killing," I said. "I realize you don't mind dying. You're not afraid of that. But I'm an ape."

"So what?" she sneered.

"We apes understand that there are many things worse than a clean quick death. We simians experience the pain of poverty, hunger, illness, and the death of our beloved children."

"Ha," she said. "You don't frighten me." There was a trace of doubt in her voice.

"That's because you don't understand pain yet. You will. I'll teach you. Now, your forearm cutting into your back hurts."

"I can take it," she said.

"Of course, you can," I said. "That's one kind of pain, but when I bend your arm higher" – I bent her arm as I spoke – "it puts a strain on your elbow and your shoulder."

She hissed.

"It has a different quality than the cutting pain," I said. "Although your shoulder muscle is quite well-developed so you can swing your arm outward, it is not nearly as strong for other movements." I continued to apply leverage as I spoke. "The joints aren't made to move in this direction."

"Bastard! Barbarian," she said.

"Oh, you don't know the half of it," I said. "Tell me who you're working for, or I will tear up your shoulder."

"Laa's family sent me," she said.

"No, they didn't," I answered. "Laa keeps track of them for me. So, let's eliminate that lie." I shoved her arm higher.

She screamed when the muscle ripped.

Any halfway sensitive being would have stopped. I continued. I wrenched her shoulder and dislocated the shoulder joint. Tears coursed down her face. My stomach twisted. I had to restrain myself from crying with her. She would interpret sympathy as weakness. I had to out-brutalize the aliens.

"That's one shoulder," I said. "Medical science is very good here, but I'm not sure how often the doctors have to deal with replacing shoulders. Can they rebuild muscles and tendons? Try again. The truth this time." I locked my feelings away, knowing I would suffer for it later.

"You don't understand what they will do to me if I tell," she said.

I steeled myself, walling off the pity I ought to have felt for her. My voice became ragged with anger, much of it directed inward.

"That's true, but what they do will come later. I'm damaging you right now. Think about how many joints you have in your upper body alone – elbows, wrists, hands and fingers. I can ruin them all, one after the other. Then I can start on your lower torso. I can leave you alive but unable to walk, unable to crawl. You'll be in constant pain. You'll have to persuade someone to dress you, feed you, and wipe your ass."

There was only one monster in this conflict, and it was me. She squirmed and rocked, but she had not trained for wrestling. Her movements cut her own back. I racked her arm more and more. She was tough and determined, but eventually, she stopped trying to escape.

"I'll tell you, but you have to promise to do me a favor," she muttered. "It won't endanger you. You couldn't be in more trouble than you are already anyway. And don't tell anyone I gave in."

"Okay," I said softly. "Speak quietly so the crowd can't overhear. I swear I will never admit you told me. You'll be remembered for bravely refusing to tell me anything at all. Your reputation as a warrior will not suffer."

"It's the royals who want you dead," she said softly. "Fez is not the only member of that family. The traditional faction says you've gone too far in upsetting the way things are. You have apes and insectoids working together. You allow other species to live in your area. You act like you are as important as the royals. You're too damned smart for an insignificant being. To them the worst thing is you refuse to kill your enemies, which encourages the religious fanatics and undermines the fear they rule by. They plan to humiliate you and prove you are a sham before they kill you. And they will. Goddamn you."

It made sense. Too much sense to be a lie.

"Okay, I believe you," I said. "What favor do you want?"

"Unlock the sleeve on my good arm," she said. "Don't worry. I swear I will not kill you. You're already dead, you just don't know it yet."

"Should I roll you to your back first to free your arm?"

"To my right side, please," she said.

"That's going to hurt a lot."

"Not for long," she said. "Tell me. Can you really beat Dob in individual combat?"

"In demonstrations, not real battles, she and I win about equally often. Contests often end in a tie. My best guess is that in a real battle both of us would die."

"That makes me feel better," she said. "I couldn't believe it when they told me that. I should have. For a worthless bag of skin and an inferior species, you have a surprising sense of honor."

I rolled her over as gently as possible. I unlocked her sleeve. She stretched out her neck. She slit her throat. Red blood flowed into the brown pools of the driver's drying blood. The two bodies rested close together. Sadness and regret settled in my heart. I'd never thought of myself as a sadist, but I had tortured the Plix to find out what I now recognized I had suspected all along. Who else had the power to kill me and an interest in my death? I sat on the mat and stared at the bodies. What did their deaths accomplish?

Doc rushed to me and grabbed my hand. "We have to go," she said, pulling me to my feet. "Someone from the Arena is bound to come and ask questions. I don't understand why someone from the audience didn't ask an official to stop this."

"Nobody was going to leave during the main event," I replied, leaning on her as I steadied myself. "The audience was thrilled. The Razors you sponsored will be talking for decades about how great this evening was. And you'll probably get a raise from the sadists back home. I hope you recorded it. The replay rights will make you wealthy from your blood-hungry superiors and their friends. All my barbarism and sadism resulted in learning nothing that I didn't already know."

85

CHAPTER FIFTEEN

"Az is here to see you," announced Laa.

The Razor shook his head as I approached.

"Did you go to the Arena last night?" he asked.

"Yes, I saw some interesting matches between the simians," I said. "I think I might ask one or two if they'd be interested in joining the guards. And then some insectoid killed an ape and threatened me, but she didn't realize I was right there. Then I left."

"Thank goodness," said Az. "In each of the outer rings an insectoid killed an ape and then threatened you aloud. If the garbled reports I got are accurate, in one ring the Plix then lost to another ape and killed herself. I was worried that you might have been involved. There aren't many apes who can handle an insectoid. You ought to recruit the winner, if you can identify him. The whole planet is buzzing about it, but nobody admits to being there. As a result, we issued a formal rule against interspecies death matches. So, you didn't see a heroic ape defeat a Plix?"

"No. I heard the threat but honestly I didn't see anything even close to a heroic ape." The truth was easier to say than I expected.

"We clarified the rule about no fighting between different species, so there is no reason to continue my research about making adjustments so you can fight evenly with an insectoid."

"I agree," I said. "I'm sorry you spent so much time looking into it."

"I'm not," said Az. "It gave me an excuse to review Arena history. I enjoyed it very much. I'm finding it surprisingly hard to wrangle you an invitation to a duel. For some reason the traditionalists are vehemently opposed, but I will keep working at it. Oh, work, that reminds me," he said. "I need to add credits to your necklace. Apparently, this area used to be a slum, but since you arrived, it's become quite popular among the commoners. And you've done other work Fez finds important. He told me to pay you."

Az let out a low whistle when he saw my chain. "That's beautiful." He touched the chain, which took on the white-gold color of palladium in an intricate woven rope design. The gem became a gorgeous black diamond the size of a walnut and the pendant ended in a sculpture of crashing waves.

He shook his head as he let the chain fall back against my chest. "Wow! I've never seen anything like this. You're as rich as any royal on the planet."

...

Laa told me another being was waiting for me.

He stood in the vestibule. He was massive and hairy. A silverback gorilla might have given him a good wrestling match.

I approached him warily.

"You don't recognize me, do you?" he asked.

"No, but there's something familiar about your voice.... Captain?"

"Yes, I'm in port and I heard about this famous human who was once a passenger of mine. I had to check it out for myself to see if that was you."

"You gave me a chance, cured my cancer, and even provided me with clothes. Thank you."

He laughed. "I don't usually have an extensive wardrobe for my guests, but the watcher at the port was kind enough to provide them for you. They didn't cost me a cent. I left him stark naked and unconscious. He was arrested the next day for indecent exposure. Whatever kindness I gave you has been repaid ten times over. Since you became Ambassador, the market in handmade terrestrial goods has skyrocketed. I have the contacts on Earth to acquire the stuff without revealing myself, which is the tricky part of the trade. I now have three ships making the run. Amazingly, the bank loaned me the money for expansion. I'm in danger of becoming one of those successful business types I like to bitch about instead of a barely-scraping-by tramp freighter captain with a steady run between fourth-rate planets."

"Is Razor Prime a fourth-rate planet?" I asked.

"You don't have any way to compare it to other places," he said. "Yeah, this planet's main income from the rest of the galaxy is from blood-sport tourists who come to watch the Razor duels. Not many want to come here. Most of the royals are terrified that any change will throw them out on their asses. They'd rather stay backward and in charge than allow everyone on the planet to advance. The royals want the different species to stay at each other's throats so they don't join together against them. When threatened, they kill their enemies to try to keep the lid on. Razor Prime is hardly a vacation paradise. Before they were sponsored, Razors were no more advanced than humans. It's ridiculous that they are allowed to sponsor any beings."

"That confirms what I've been told by others," I said.

"I was really surprised that you made it to the Capital, but the fact that you are still alive is truly amazing," said the Captain.

"Well, they'll correct that mistake soon, I'm sure," I said.

...

Shortly after my conversation with Az, Laa entered. She was accompanied by Hy, dragging his left leg that was wrapped in a bandage. His face was cut and bruised. They shoved an unhappy-looking Razor ahead of them. He was the first and only obese Razor I ever saw. He had an expression like an indolent student called to the principal's office.

"What happened to you, Hy?" I asked.

"I'll explain later," he said. "Deal with this one first."

"I am an attorney associated with what you would call the planetary bank," the stranger said. "These two suggested I come to you, as if you might be someone I need to deal with."

"Show him your necklace," said Laa. I removed it from around my neck. The Razor's eyes widened. He bounced from foot to foot.

"If you check your records you will find that Conner is an important stakeholder in your institution," said Laa. "I am, too, but on a much smaller scale."

"Oh, *that* Conner," the Razor said. "I recognize the name. I have been curious. Your investments have soared. I admit I laughed when you bought extensive cheap property around the embassy, but improvements in the infrastructure and housing have increased the value immensely. Setting up an area where different species coexist in peace at the same time rioting happens almost everywhere else opened the housing market to many more bidders. It's gone from a slum to a highly desirable area. You keep buying property on the outskirts of what you own and doing it all again. It is the act of a genius. You created a brand-new market. The return on investment is relatively small compared to other real estate transactions in terms of absolute amounts, but the percentage of gain is incredible and the volume is steadily increasing."

I looked over at Laa, who was apparently admiring the ceiling and smiling. She was, of course, the mastermind.

The lawyer continued. "Your investments in small businesses in the area – artisans, bookkeepers, factories, and so forth – result in creating your own loyal customers. More genius. Even your willingness to loan to a tramp freighter captain who was barely making ends meet worked out. The cumulative income is truly breathtaking."

Laa hummed under her breath and refused to catch my eye.

"If you were to write up your methods, I'm sure you could sell millions of books. Do you know that all by yourself you have changed the entire conception of ape-men?"

"Thanks, but right now I want to put my affairs in order," I said. "I trust you can assist me with that."

"Of course," said the lawyer. "With the coming change in government, that is wise. I can assure you that whatever happens with the royals, the bank will protect your interests and honor your wishes. We predate the royals, and we will continue long after they are forgotten. Shall we proceed?"

...

After the lawyer left, Hy explained, "Fez is missing. Royals are fighting each other for the first time in history. Most in Fez's progressive faction are dead or in hiding. The traditionalists are in power but many of them died in the melee. It's an unstable situation. My men fought a holding action while Fez escaped."

"You are the most visible reminder of the progressive program," said Laa. "They will come for you probably to make an example of what horrors come from anything less than blind allegiance to the past."

It wasn't a surprise, but it hurt to hear it. "I never expected to last as long as I have. Thanks for the warning. I don't see any point in running. Where would I go? Who would help me? I'll prepare the best I can."

"Your guards will fight for you," said Hy. "I can help Dob set up defenses and traps. We can turn the entire district into a fortified killing ground."

I looked at the earnest expressions on their faces and felt a surge of affection and respect. They were willing to die to protect me.

"Thank you," I said. "I am grateful and honored by your suggestions. But the killing ground would kill guards and neighbors who I love. This island of peace would become a battleground, destroying what we have built together. I said I would not kill sentients. I will not order my friends to kill or to face their deaths either. That is final." I put my hand up palm outward to fend off further discussion. "Make it absolutely clear to everyone that when the royal guards come for me, there will be no opposition."

"I'm going to prepare," I said to Laa. "I would appreciate it if you and Doc came with me."

"You think it will happen today?" she asked.

"Why would they wait?" I asked. "The outcome is uncertain so they have to take action. It feels like back on earth when a thunderstorm is about to break. Make it clear. I do not want the guards to oppose the royal troops in any way."

CHAPTER SIXTEEN

I put on the clothing I wore when I got off the spaceship, ate a light meal, and put a few thoughts on paper while I waited. Ten royal guards showed up shortly after sundown. My security force would have easily overwhelmed several times their number but they did not. My guards stood at ease. I did not recognize the royal officer. His sergeant carried heavy chains.

"You won't need those," I said, pointing at the restraints. "I imagine ten royal guards can manage one unarmed human and two escorts. But perhaps you are as afraid of me as the royals in charge are."

The officer gestured. The sergeant dropped the chains.

I turned toward my guards. "I cannot tell you how proud I am of each and every one of you. I arrived on the planet alone and friendless. You have made me feel welcome. Although I am an alien, you accepted me in your hearts. Together we created a home that is safe and open to all species. As my last request of you, I ask that you keep it that way. Hard times are coming. I will not be here to guide you. But I have trust and faith that you will maintain this area as we together created it." Tears filled my eyes. I was too choked up to continue. I nodded to the officer and we headed toward the Arena.

It was a clear night. I looked up at the constellations of stars that were so different from what I used to see at home. The crowd around the Arena parted silently as we passed through. I waved to a few beings I knew and smiled at the youngsters who called out my name.

Inside we walked to one of the central rings. Beings were already seated around the ring. The noise level increased when they saw me. Waving and bowing, I turned to every section of the audience. Scattered applause followed. I spotted some familiar faces and went to sit with the Master, Az, and Dob. The beings next to them made space for me, Laa, and Doc.

"This is a total disgrace," said the Master. "I refused to fight to represent the royal family. I just made a rule outlawing duels between members of different species. You must have a terrible opinion of the Arena and I cannot blame you."

"Any institution can be abused," I said. "I understand you are not responsible." An announcer stepped to the middle of the ring and spoke. The acoustics were superb. His voice carried to all parts of the Arena.

"Gentle beings, welcome to the first night of a new era of enlightened and wholesome governance by a new coalition of royal family members who are going to make this world glorious again. Razor Prime for Razors! No more bad-smelling aliens defecating in the streets and ruining the day by their hideous appearance. No more unsavory mixing with inferiors in your neighborhoods."

He stopped, apparently expecting applause, but he got less response than I had received earlier. Maybe the new administration did not yet have the hearts and minds of the audience.

"I realize you didn't come to hear me speak, melodic as my voice is. You came to witness the new order exemplified by our own royal Fye, who will rid us of a major annoyance and irritant: the alien, Conner."

I acted as though I was startled and pointed to myself as if surprised. "Who? Me?" I said.

The audience laughed.

"Keep it up," whispered Laa. "This is not what Fye expected. In the past victors carried the severed heads of the defeated around the ring, but Fez escaped. This is a poor substitute."

The announcer scurried over to introduce Fye, who was dressed in a dazzling white form-fitted one-piece outfit with purple trim. It looked like it had been tailored to make him look muscular, but the tailor had not entirely succeeded. Fye started with a windy speech full of self-praise and overblown claims. Then he came to the current event. "You will see for yourselves the ugly alien flee from me like the coward that he is, that all aliens are. Oh, he may be clever and try to turn the tables on me. He's a sneaky one."

Dob murmured, "They reinstated me and ordered me to tell them about your fighting style. I warned him about your ability to sneak inside his guard and cautioned him about slashing widely."

Fye said, "I have to warn you that it may take some time for me to track him down. The poor thing has no ability to attack, only defend."

Dob continued, "I told him that I've always seen you counterattack, never initiate the action. In my experience, you never leave your feet until after your opponent is down."

Fye then said, "Perhaps the most pathetic thing about him is his insistence that he is not willing to kill. He's like some misbegotten religious zealots on this planet. They should observe what happens to him and remember they may be next. He has no moral or ethical principles. Maybe he has a weak stomach. More likely, he's such a poor excuse for a warrior that he never gets the chance. Don't be swayed by his pleading and whimpering. He will meet his end tonight."

"After I gave away all your secrets," said Dob, "they cashiered me a second time from the guards."

"Thanks for the information, Dob," I said. "It's hard to believe they were stupid enough to kick out a great warrior twice."

I turned to Doc. "Here is a being like the ones you chose to sponsor – the ones worth your instruction and tender care as they slaughter the innocent and the worthless. Well, you have a good seat for the entertainment. I'll try to bleed enough not to disappoint you high and mighty godlings." She looked away and did not respond. Her color changed to white. I remembered that in Japan white is the color for mourning.

I motioned for the announcer to come to me. He refused and I exaggerated my gestures. The crowd booed him when he turned away. I held up one finger. Finally, he relented and came over.

"I only have one question for you: How does Fye clean his boots when you're not around to lick them for him?" The crowd exploded into laughter and cheers.

Fye marched to the middle of the ring and gestured for me to come to him.

"Jimmy, before we start, tell me why your species dies when their host does."

It's usually unexpected. The body of the host shuts down and we are trapped inside.

"What if the host knew when he was going to die and expelled you?" I asked mentally. "You lived independently when we met. Can you survive outside another body again?"

I stood and sauntered toward Fye.

I suppose so. I'm not very big. I'd need help not to be trampled.

"You can communicate with Laa," I thought. "She would help you. I might die here. You don't have to. Come to my mouth during the fight and I'll spit you out if I think I'm going down."

Fye kept his elbows against his body like the other Razor I had faced. It made him look like a penguin. It severely limited the range of his slashes. He couldn't cover his head above his nose. I charged him. Apparently, he thought it was a feint until I reached over his guard and slapped his face. He stepped back, blinking his eyes. I dove at his ankles and knocked him off his feet. He landed on his back. If he had stayed that way, he would have been dangerous to attack. However, he went to his hands and knees. I swung behind him and put him in an ankle lock, staying far enough away that he could not reach me with his razor-sharp outer forearms. Next, facing away from his head, I straddled him and raised his legs off the floor, which extended his body, and then I leaned back. In professional wrestling, the hold is called "The Boston Crab." Fye yelped immediately. Tears came to his eyes. The hold is a submission move, but I was not about to let him submit.

"This is the Razor who will return you to glory," I announced to the crowd. "Show us your courage, Fye. Defy me while I rip your knees to shreds."

"No, please don't," he begged.

"What? Are you begging for mercy from me, an inferior?"

"Yes. Please don't hurt me. Please don't kill me," he howled.

"This was supposed to be a long match," I said. "I hope nobody went out for popcorn."

Applause and cheering followed my statement. "Do you see how pathetic he is? By himself, he is a coward. He's a royal, which means he has others do his fighting. He has others do his killing. If they refuse, if all of you refuse, he is the same as any of you, except that he is more of a coward."

I increased the pressure. He yelled louder.

"Understand one thing," I said. "I could easily kill him, but I do not kill."

I felt Jimmy in my throat. In a second, I spat him out of my mouth, mentally wishing him a long and prosperous life.

CHAPTER SEVENTEEN

To finish Conner's story: Conner let Fye go. He helped the royal to his feet. Then the earthman stood unmoving, facing his opponent, showing no fear. Fye, shaking and red in the face, slit Conner's throat. Apparently, Fye attempted to cut Conner's head off. I imagine he intended to carry it around the ring like the ancients did after they defeated their foes. Beings in the crowd stormed from the stands. I sent my location to Laa, who ran to grab a handful of Conner's spit with me in it. Fye went down under the angry mob, never to rise again. The rebellion started that continues to this day.

...

I decided that Conner should be remembered. For the past two years, I have tried to write his story in the way I think Conner would have told it. When I was inside him and he did not need my skills, I rummaged around in his memories. He was a fascinating creature. I came to understand his life as he experienced it.

Oh, I should mention that Conner had emancipated Laa long before that night. He told Fez he would accept her indenture. And he did. He didn't say he would keep her indentured.

Since the night Conner died, Razor Prime has been in a political uproar. The neighborhood now revered as Conner's Embassy has beaten off every attempt to destroy it. Avians patrol the sky while widebodies with natural armor protect the Avian nests well inside the borders. The expanded guard forces watch for trouble. The most reckless rioters died. The rest have learned to direct their attention elsewhere. Dob and Laa command the neighborhood forces. Fez appeared about six months ago, looking battered and bruised. He asked for asylum, and it was granted after he renounced all political power and donated ninety percent of his money to Conner's Embassy. He lives quietly and has no role in the community. Nobody knows who will end up in charge, but it won't be like it was. My guess is the few surviving royals will end with a symbolic role and quite limited power.

Doc's people shifted their governance, too. Doc explained that the former leaders were disgraced and expelled from authority forever but not executed. Conner destabilized every entrenched power he came in contact with.

Doc's race ended the Razors' sponsorship of the earth. They now sponsor humans directly. With the help of the Conner Foundation created in his will, they disseminate medical information, non-polluting energy, drinkable water, food, and educational opportunities all over Earth. I am honored to act as one of the judges for the Conner Awards, which recognize extraordinary acts of peacemaking throughout the known universe. The monetary value of the award exceeds the Nobel Prize awards.

As his reputation spreads, Liam Conner continues to inspire beings throughout the galaxy. Pilgrims come to Razor Prime to visit the dock where he landed, the Embassy where he lived, and the Arena where he sacrificed himself. All are under the protection of Conner's guards. The Captain allows two passengers per trip from Earth to Razor Prime to retrace Conner's path on his ship, one in each cabin Conner lived in. Pilgrims go to Earth to visit Conner's former residences, the jail cells he occupied, and the courtroom where he offered to fight the bullies. The Campbell Hematologic Malignancies Clinic infusion lab isn't needed for the treatment of cancer anymore. It is now a museum.

BONUS STORIES

BUFFALO SOLDIERS DAY

"Why the hell should I have plans for Buffalo Soldiers Day?" asked Tyrell Carney, glaring at me through narrowed eyes. His nostrils flared. Then his face changed as he clamped down on his anger.

His loud voice alerted people in the office something was going on. People were too polite to stare, but I was certain everyone was listening.

In a softer voice he continued, "Mr. Williams, don't take this wrong. I am not angry at you. I'm grateful you hired me right out of law school. Williams, Johnson and Davis does more civil rights law than any other firm in South Carolina. I am delighted to be here."

"I'm glad to hear you say so," I said. "When you think I'm wrong about something, I want you to tell me like you just did. Honest disagreement leads us to better practice of the law. So, what made you angry? I sincerely want to know."

Carney sighed.

"Sir, Buffalo Soldiers Day memorializes how some black men got the right to vote. Most us of did not. Personally, I do not find it to be a reason for celebration. More than a million Negroes took part in the Second World War, but the armed services are still segregated. Baseball finally allowed one Negro to play first base, but he can't vote. On Buffalo Soldiers Day I plan to grit my teeth and work harder so eventually I can work for the right of all men to vote."

"I'm sorry. I didn't understand," I said. "Of course, as a white man I can only guess what it is like for Negroes in America. It has

100

never made sense to me why people should have lousy schools, separate bathrooms, or should have to step into the gutter because of their race. The implications of Hitler's Aryan super race made my convictions stronger. My son was a navigator in a B-29 during the war. He told me he only survived thanks to the Red Tail fighter escorts flown by the Tuskegee Airmen. I resolved then and there to do everything I could for the men who fought and died for a country that still treats them so cruelly. State politics are getting worse. Give me a chance to change it and I will."

We shook hands. Carney took two steps and then my assistant, Amber Herbert, stopped him. She was close enough for me to catch a whiff of her perfume, a subtle hint of magnolia. I couldn't help overhearing them.

"Mr. Carney, how many white men celebrate Buffalo Soldiers Day? And, of the few, how many are happy President Grant was able to salvage one shining dream from Abraham Lincoln – to give the vote to Union colored troops, other prominent colored men, and their descendants?"

"Very few, I imagine."

She put her hands on her hips.

"Did your law school mention the amendment allows other black men plus their descendants to become voters when enough states agree? It rarely happens, but it is possible."

Carney nodded.

Her eyes flashed. "Do you realize how much the man you lectured has done for us?"

"Miss Amber, he is a good man. As I told him, I am honored to be working alongside him. Please excuse me. I have work to do."

I hoped he was aware Amber had studiously ignored him since his first day with us – a sure sign she was interested in him.

Helen Carter, the retired principal of Frederick Douglass who volunteered in the office, drifted toward me. "You might take into account that he got a letter from Reliable Eligibility Associates this morning. I noticed it in his mailbox."

My face flushed and my pulse accelerated.

"Goddamn, the REA. Amber, Helen, we need to take a hard look at them."

...

A week later, Amber opened the door to my office and peeked in. "I realize you left directions not to be disturbed, but Pastor Luke called and wanted to talk. I think you should speak to him."

I stood up and stretched. My back ached from being hunched over my desk poring over the results of legal actions against Reliable Eligibility Associates. I blinked my watery eyes.

"When I have a second free, I'll call him."

"No need."

The phone on my desk rang. I picked up the receiver and spoke into it. "Pastor Luke."

"My favorite white man," said a man with a rich baritone voice.

"Is that a compliment? I'm not sure."

Laughter came through the phone.

"Of course, it is. I'm calling to offer my assistance. My congregants tell me you're looking at ancestry searches performed by Reliable Eligibility Associates. I'm curious and I want to help. In fact, REA looked into the possibility that one of my ancestors fought in the Civil War. I hoped I might have a connection that would make me eligible to vote. As you are aware, I have the largest black congregation in the state. I can arrange press coverage and radio interviews at any time I want. So, what's up?"

I thought for a moment.

"You can definitely help," I said. "You have the loudest horn outside the walls of Jericho, but Joshua didn't rush in first thing. You sometimes talk about living on the edge of the lions' den. It could be that there will be a lion hunt coming. I don't want to alert the lions until everything is ready."

"So?"

"So, Pastor, when your people ask you about it, I'd appreciate it if you would encourage their involvement in issues about health care, education, and jobs. There is no certainty that what I'm working on will pan out. If it does, I don't know for certain if it will work in a court, or when it will work at all."

"Are you including me in your advice?" he growled.

"Heavens, no," I said. "I trust your good judgment. And I need information about your experience with REA. Why did you choose them?"

"I may have been foolish, but their ads on television said they were the first licensed company in the state."

"That's true," I said.

"They say they've done more research and gotten more men enrolled as voters than any other ancestry firm."

"Also true," I said.

"They promised to spend as many hours as needed to investigate my background completely for a fixed fee."

I blinked.

"Was the promise in writing?" I asked.

"I think so," said Pastor Luke. "It was some years back so I don't recall the exact wording. Is this important?"

My chest felt lighter.

"It might be. I would really like to take a look at every scrap of paper you have from them. How soon can you locate what you have and send it to me?"

"I'm at church now. I'll need to go home to look for it."

"Please do. Oh, and can you contact other people in the church who hired REA back then? If the applicants have died since they put in their requests, can you ask their families to search for the records?"

"It sounds like you have the bit in your teeth now. God bless you, brother. Bye."

"I'll call his wife," said Amber. "She'll find what you want before he gets home to mess up their records."

...

Later in the week, I called a meeting in my office to discuss progress to date.

"Principal Carter, why don't you start?" I said.

"I'll begin with some history to give perspective. On April 4, 1865, two days after the Confederate army abandoned Richmond, Virginia, Abraham Lincoln and his son, Tad, visited the city. The boat they had ridden in later hit a mine, killing everyone on board. In Lincoln's memory, amendments abolishing slavery and awarding citizenship to blacks were enacted fairly quickly. Suffrage, however, was not passed until seventy years ago. Lincoln intended to limit the eligible men so the amendment would pass and the men would serve as a wedge to expand later."

I nodded.

"The state legislature licensed one firm, Reliable Eligibility Associates, to evaluate family heritage and pass on to Congress the names of the male progeny of the enfranchised. The firm was founded by scallywags and carpetbaggers – the former Confederate officers and northern reformers who came to educate families of the formerly enslaved. The founders and subsequent generations of their families ran the operation honestly until ten years ago, when it was sold."

"Who owns it now?" I asked.

"The company is now a partnership made up of the rising Dixiecrats. The boneheaded older generation was made up of at least honest political Neanderthals. Not this new lot."

Amber nodded and spoke. "Immediately the new owners set up impossible quotas for staff. When they didn't reach them, they quit or got fired. The company brought on new staff, mostly relatives, who had no experience or qualifications. Now their reports are full of we-promise-nothing boilerplate clauses. It would take less than half an hour to churn out one of their reports. The findings are so similar REA could print them out in purple ink on mimeographs if they didn't mind the smell. However, the owners used the contracts from the previous regime for close to two years. Apparently, they used up the printed forms on hand until they were all gone."

I smiled. "I love going up against the combination of greed and stupidity in legal proceedings. We have a sound civil suit against them for bad faith and overcharging on their current contracts. Please see how many people they've ripped off who we can add to the action. Their hold-harmless crap might work with some clients, but Pastor Luke and his older friends have rock-solid contracts. I'm working on a criminal complaint, and I have two examples of malfeasance, but I believe there are more. Investigators in Columbia and Washington, D.C., would listen and put me on their waiting list, but it would be some time before they could deal with the matter. I don't have the political pull to demand their attention right away. Excellent work, you two. We've got enough to start writing the pleadings."

After they left, I rubbed my forehead, feeling a headache coming on. I wanted to do more than simply embarrass the REA partners. I wanted more repercussions than negative publicity and fines.

A receptionist rang me.

"Mr. Sam Brown is on the line. He claims you'll want to talk to him."

"I do indeed," I said. "Put him through."

"Daniel, I need to thank you," Sam said. "You saved me. Your politics may be Communist-tinged, but your instincts are spot on."

His voice brought back memories of his cigar smoke-filled office.

"How did I save your super-reactionary ass this time, Sam?" I asked.

"You warned me the young Dixiecrats would set me up for a fall. And they did. When my personal secretary retired, one of the applicants for her position came to the interview, crossed her legs, and showed me her religion right then and there."

"Spare me the details, Sam, please."

"Suffice it to say, I remembered your warning. I shooed her out and eventually traced the honey trap to one of my assistants, who is now making personal inspections of the worst prisons and substandard housing units."

"A member of the new Klan brand of Dixiecrats on the way up. Right, Sam?"

"I wouldn't use that label," he said. "Not in public anyway."

"Those snakes are vicious, but stupid, right?" I asked.

"I have a stump in my backyard with a higher IQ than any of them."

I smiled and asked, "If one of them took your position as attorney general of South Carolina, would you be comfortable with that?"

I listened to Sam breathe over the phone line. I rubbed my forehead, holding my headache at bay while I waited for his answer. Twenty seconds passed like an hour.

"Not...not entirely, but my days as a political leader are over. I have no influence on the new party members. I hoped I could keep them inside the tent pissing out instead of them standing outside pissing into it. My plans didn't work. I won't run for re-election."

"Did they know when they set the trap?" I asked.

"Yep," he said with sadness in his voice.

"That's really nasty. They'd ruin your reputation forever simply because they don't want to wait a year and a half until the end of your term. They're so cold they could freeze the balls off a pool table."

Sam chortled.

"So, tell me, Sam, how do you want to be remembered? You could be remembered as a man of honor who opposed injustice without regard for privilege or politics."

...

Five days later, Carney showed up at my office.

"You sent for me, sir?" His voice was steady but his hands were jammed into his pockets and the expression on his face looked like a cloudy day.

"Yes, please close the door and take a seat," I said. "Mr. Carney, you look like a student who's been called to the principal's office. You're not in trouble. I want to tell you before you hear on the news about the FBI in conjunction with the state Attorney General's office investigating Reliable Eligibility Associates."

Carney tilted his head.

"They are?"

"Although you don't know it, you were the catalyst for the investigation."

His eyes widened.

"I apologize, Mr. Carney. I have been less than entirely honest with you. I have never lied to you, but I have not told you about things you might be interested in knowing. When you applied to the firm, I was impressed you worked full time and attended law school at night. You showed unusual dedication and persistence. And I was intrigued by your name. I'm a Lincoln admirer. So, without telling you, I had an ancestry evaluation of your family completed."

I put up the palms of my hands.

"Let me absolutely assure you I did not violate your personal privacy. A careful search of public domain records revealed your great-great-grandfather was Sergeant William Carney. He was the first member of the Union colored infantry to be awarded the Medal of Honor. He carried the flag for the 54th Massachusetts regiment during the assault on Fort Wagner. He led the troops forward despite multiple wounds."

Carney blinked rapidly and then stared at me.

"My ancestor was a Buffalo soldier?"

"More than a soldier, he was a hero. The one battle did a great deal to convince both sides in the war that Negroes were as brave as whites. I had intended to surprise you with the information on Buffalo Soldiers Day."

He blinked.

"So, the finding by REA was false," said Carney.

"Totally," I said. "You qualify for voting. You described the report to Helen back when it arrived. She told me. It confirmed rumors I'd heard for some time. The REA fraudulently took your money, pretended to research family histories, and falsely advised you they were not eligible to vote. They pulled the same shenanigans on many other Negroes. I apologize for not telling you sooner. I should have said something immediately. I got completely wrapped up in gathering information about their scam, but it does not excuse my behavior."

"I accept your apology. I'm stunned," said Carney. "Thank you."

"I can give you the ancestry report and the registration form to become certified," I said. "Here's a letter of support from South Carolina's Attorney General. You don't need it but it should speed up the response."

Carney nodded.

"The Dixiecrat Governor wants to distance himself from party members who own the firm," I said. "He claims he wasn't aware of what they were doing. I actually believe him. He backs segregation less blatantly than that. He'll announce support for all pending requests for suffrage from individual Negro men who have applied under the constitutional amendment President Grant got passed. The legislature will concur to save face. It's a small step for a few, but it's something."

Carney's eyes glistened with tears.

"This will renew efforts to enfranchise all Negro men," he said. "It will be in the headlines all across the nation."

"And one more thing," I said.

"What?"

"Mr. Carney, you're going to need an attorney for your civil action against the REA owners. I would say the chances are good you will end up a rich man. I'd be honored if you would consider hiring me."

SECOND SECOND CHANCE

I awoke in confusion. I experienced the usual sensations that followed time travel – a fading memory of dreaming I was flying, the taste of grapefruit on my tongue, and tingling in my fingertips and toes. But something was very wrong. Where was I? When was I? My mission was to help Dolly Madison haul valuables out of the White House before the British set it on fire. The major American treasure I was sent to protect was of course Dolly herself. I expected to be in the city of Washington on August 24th, 1814.

Instead, I was in the wrong place and at the wrong time. I lay concealed in the underbrush, wearing a green uniform like a handful of other soldiers nearby. They cursed the colonists who were revolting against their rightful king. Their accents and vocabulary sounded like the English working class in the late 1700s.

The commander, a man with bright red hair, snarled at us, "Shut your bone boxes." He was clearly Scottish.

I held an amazingly sophisticated breech-loading flintlock weapon with a rifled barrel. That plus the appearance of the commander let me guess the time and place.

I remembered that in late 1777, or maybe it was 1778, Major Patrick Ferguson, a Scotsman, known as the finest shot in the British army, commanded a small force of expert marksmen. To locate colonial forces, they took cover close to Brandywine Creek in Pennsylvania, where they monitored a major roadway.

My memory proved correct when a cavalry officer dressed in the flamboyant uniform of a European hussar rode into view, followed by an American officer wearing a high-cocked hat. The British soldiers had no way of knowing who the men were, but I knew – Count Casimir Pulaski from Poland and General George Washington.

Ferguson signaled for me and two other men to move forward. One man moved with the grace of a serpent, not disturbing the underbrush or giving any hint of his passage. The second man grimaced and moved stiffly, as though in pain. His face was bruised. Without orders, he got into a shooting position. I slid next to the second man and pulled his hand away from the rifle.

"Don't move, Aevum," I whispered.

He stared at me and struggled to free his hand. I held it immobile, aware of the sounds of passing hoofbeats nearby.

"You're injured. You couldn't take me if you weren't. You cannot both fight me and carry out your assignment. Your opportunity is gone."

His eyes narrowed, but he didn't move. Ferguson motioned us to return. As we made our way back, Ferguson stood. He shouted at the colonial officer. Washington looked back. He touched his hat in respect before cantering slowly away. Ferguson spared Washington's life. In the near future, Pulaski would save the future president.

The would-be assassin and I remained locked in that moment of time while time continued for the soldiers. From their point of view we had never been present.

"Tempus, Pilgrim, you cannot protect the American status quo against the will of the people," hissed the would-be assassin. "Your reluctance to spill blood leaves you weak and useless."

"The status quo is change," I said. "Painfully slow change, I admit. The wealthy continue to get richer and try to lock out the have-nots. We work with time to improve the state of the nation. Violence only begets more violence. The person who hates his slumlord and sets his apartment building on fire might hurt the building's owner financially, but he definitely hurts all the tenants."

The revolutionist smiled. "If it hurts enough, the residents join our cause."

I shook my head. "Except various Aevum groups have different goals. You squabble over trivial disagreements, while big issues get ignored."

He did not respond.

I continued. "Your numbers are dwindling. How many set out on this mission? You made it through, but you were injured in the process. You probably won't make it back. Besides, what would killing Washington accomplish? Do you have some plan for what follows? Change might make things even worse."

"Fine words," he spat. "Maybe they are not entirely false. Five of us were willing to give up our lives. You lose people too. What does your way accomplish beyond delaying real change?"

I thought about the Pilgrims on the Edmund Pettis Bridge in Selma, Alabama, on Bloody Sunday in 1965. Did our sacrifices add anything to the courage and dignity of those who tried to cross?

"Tell me, Tempus, would you have killed me if I had aimed at Washington?"

Time intervened. We were swept apart before I was able to answer.

Of course, no two people experience time travel the same way. I never remember thoughts, sounds, or sights. For me, after a short period of disorientation and queasiness, it's sort of like swimming. Instinctively, I ease into the current, which carries me along and deposits me safely, tired but exhilarated. The landing pad is a comfortable room in the secret army base where images of fish swim along the walls and soft American folk music plays in the background.

I awoke stretched out on a faded tan lounge chair. My clothing had not survived to modern times, just as all items from the present revert to the raw form they had in the past.

I rushed to the door and opened it.

"I need to debrief ASAP," I yelled as I headed toward officer territory.

Second Lieutenant Margaret O'Donnell saw me coming and eyed me up and down. She blushed. So did I. I had forgotten to put on a robe. Seeing her in uniform would be more than reason enough for any man to enlist.

"Any time you want me for a close personal inspection, Margaret, just let me know. Right now I've gotta see the CO."

Doctor Nasser, who had been apparently interrupted by the

noise, approached me and grabbed my arm. "What happened, Ben?"

Doc sounded more pissed off than usual. I looked up at him. He was ten inches taller than me. He leaned down toward me like a gaunt hawk watching a sparrow.

"I went on one mission but ended up in another entirely different time and place. I stopped an Aevum Revolutionist from killing George Washington."

"Completely impossible. Tell me exactly what happened."

"Other people need to know too, Doc. Let me borrow your cell phone. The general needs to find out."

...

I walked toward the conference room, fully dressed this time. I stopped at the Wall of Honor where each Pilgrim who died on a mission had been commemorated. I knew them all. I stopped before each photo, remembering them in a way very few people could. I was the last active Pilgrim of the first group trained. Four people left the program to do other things. Five were on the wall. Twelve people who trained after I did were also memorialized on the wall.

Major General Wayne Porter, who ran the meeting, looked more like a reference librarian than a stereotypical general. He was a thin man with wire-rimmed glasses and a soft voice. His golden skin color showed his mixed ancestry.

"Thank you for your report, Ben. It seems to me that you've answered all the questions you could answer. As I told you before this mission, you are officially retired as a Pilgrim. Under no circumstances will you go on another mission."

I started to speak, but he interrupted me.

"My decision is final. I've let you talk me into sending you back into a crisis way too many times. You're a civilian so I cannot give you orders. But the rest of the staff answers to me directly. You are now an instructor. Your personal experience will be invaluable in training others."

I was aware I'd been playing Russian Roulette and that I was lucky to have survived. But living on the razor's edge had made me feel intensely alive.

"Now to other matters," said the man in charge. "Dr. Nasser has asked to address the group. Most of you understand that Matthew Nasser, M.D., Ph.D., deserves credit for developing time travel."

"Sir...." started Nasser.

"Doctor, you credit others for their contributions. But you were the person who put the pieces together and made it work. "

Nasser glanced at me, raising his eyebrows.

"You all realize I was a revolutionist," said Nasser. "I helped write the equations and build the machines to pierce the flow and send people back through time. I was angry at what I perceived as the American Dream denied to minorities and immigrants. When I started to share my anger online, I found others who wanted to overthrow the powers that be. I wrote an aggressive equation that stabbed at time and forced an opening that people can claw through to reach time past. I intended to use brute force to make American culture live up to its ideals." He closed his eyes.

Porter glanced at his watch and opened his mouth. I shook my head. The general stayed silent.

"I was naïve," said the doctor. "Violence begets violence. Islamic clerics declared me a traitor to my faith. They pronounced a fatwa; I am to be killed when I am located. Dozens died before I finally faced the truth. Perhaps hundreds have died since. We tried to compel time to do our bidding through violence. How arrogant. How stupid. I betrayed the brave men and women who risked their lives for their beliefs.

"I brought everything I had to Tempus. I expected to be executed for my crimes. But you showed me mercy. Your scientists showed me how they cooperate with time. No coercion. They work toward time's goals. I still want America to change faster than it does, but time moves as time moves."

Porter took off his glasses and polished them as he spoke.

"Doctor, you discovered how we can travel in time. You improved our equations. Time reacted to the attacks from the initial approach. It improved its defenses. Revolutionists believing time was an enemy made themselves into time's enemy. Every attack resulted in better counter-measures that are increasingly dangerous to instigators. Time does not bend easily toward chaos. Attacks that fail cannot be repeated.

"We estimate the Aevum success rate of accessing the past is now down to under ten percent and falling. Of those who reach the past, virtually none of them return to the present. We are successful in attaining a time and place almost ninety percent of the time. Of course, we have no control over what happens during a mission. We recover everyone who manages to survive."

"But I have so much to atone for," said Nasser. "Yes, I am impatient and impossible to please, but there must be more I can do. Whatever the risk, I want to go on a mission."

"You are aware of the problems with that," said O'Donnell. "We've learned from harsh experience that we lose Pilgrims who don't blend in exceptionally well with the people of the era they enter. Even with their extensive research, unremarkable appearance, and careful speech patterns, they can easily stand out. We send them into inherently dangerous situations. Some of them die."

She glanced at me.

"Look at Ben, Doctor. He's five feet five inches tall and immensely strong. His coloring and features blend in. He's a talented linguist and a master at improvisation. You're six feet four inches tall. You have a beard and your face is distinctive."

"You mean I look like a brute," said Nasser. "I realize how ugly I am."

"You admit you are more obsessive than flexible," said the lieutenant. "You think profoundly but not rapidly. We might insert you once into a particular time and place, but you would never return. So many of our people went on missions to the past and never returned."

"Doc, I know you're willing to die," said the general. "But we need you here to figure out why for the first time ever a Pilgrim prepared for one mission ended up with a different one."

"Time is not God," said Nasser. "Time does not assign missions. We do. Time cannot intervene directly with individuals."

I spoke up. "Doctor, but God is greater than our understanding of the Divine. Perhaps time is a part of God. Maybe when the need is great enough Allah works through an individual person such as he did with the prophet Muhammad."

Porter cleared his throat. "Our intelligence operatives report increasing chaos and reluctance to carry out missions by Aevum groups. The groups are turning on each other in frustration over their inability to accomplish anything in the past. The good news is that only a few isolated and hardened radicals are willing to even try any more. The bad news that we can no longer discover the plans of those solitary few."

"What if time is now virtually free from attacks?" asked O'Connell. "Is it possible that time has become aware and active enough to independently push toward changes it desires?"

I sat back in my chair, thinking she might be onto something extremely important. If time wanted to try to change anything in American history, what would it attempt to alter? And how?

...

I woke up perplexed. I had a fading memory of dreaming about flying, again my tongue held the taste of grapefruit, and my fingertips and toes tingled. I must have time-traveled but without preparation. No launch pad with scientists monitoring computers. No sophisticated mechanism nicknamed Mr. Peabody's Wayback Machine. Time plucked me from the meeting and dropped me...when and where?

I found myself driving a new black open barouche model carriage pulled by a matched team of elegant bay Morgan horses.

"Damn it, time," I muttered. "You give me clothing, a carriage, and horses. Would it be so hard to include a newspaper?"

I could figure this out. I was fashionably dressed for a driver in new clothing. From my recollections of paintings and early forms of photography, I guessed the clothes fit roughly from the 1850s through the 1870s. Due to my preparations for the Dolly Madison mission, it was easy to recognize that I was in the busy streets of Washington city. It was a later edition of the city of Washington than the British plundered. The Smithsonian tower showed damage from a fire recent enough that only preliminary repairs showed. The Capitol Dome was visible, with a copper Statue of Freedom so new that it had not yet acquired a patina. Unfortunately, I didn't remember enough history for that to be helpful. Soldiers dressed in blue Union uniforms moved purposefully through the streets. Okay, that meant post-1861. Quite a few of the soldiers were black, and white civilians seemed used to seeing black soldiers. Therefore, it had to be later than the middle of 1862, probably later than 1863. People seemed in a celebratory mood, which was unusual during the terrible Civil War until close to the very end. Putting it all together had to be...

Time slowed. Events that happened in seconds rolled by in what I experienced as slow motion. Nasser suddenly appeared inside the carriage, dressed in an ill-fitting black suit. A handsome man sprang to the side of the carriage, extended a derringer inside, and shot the doctor in his temple.

The shooter whirled to the ground shouting, "Sic semper tyrannis!" It was all very dramatic until I flung myself from the carriage to smash my boots into the back of John Wilkes Booth's head. We both landed in the mud. He shook me off with ease. He rose to his feet and swung at me. I ducked his jab. I kicked the side of his knee. He staggered but did not fall.

Someone shouted, "He killed the President." Soldiers came running.

"Murderer," I yelled.

Booth struggled, freeing himself from two soldiers before he was overwhelmed and disappeared under a pile of cursing men.

I bent forward at the waist, breathing hard.

"My passenger looks like Old Abe but thank God, he was not the President."

...

In a moment time might sweep me away again. I wonder if it will return me to the landing pad in whatever the present is now. But I doubt it. Is there a landing pad? Does the Tempus Pilgrims program even exist?

Certainly, more assassins will attempt to kill the sixteenth president. Reconstruction after the Civil War will need a great deal of help. Time might want my help further back in the past. I'm looking forward to the future – my future – whatever it may be.

ABOUT THE AUTHOR

Warren Bull is an award-winning author with more than a hundred short stories in publication. He is the author of three novels: *Abraham Lincoln for the Defense, Abraham Lincoln in Court and Campaign,* and *Heartland*. His short story collections are *Murder Manhattan Style, Killer Eulogy and Other Stories,* and *No Happy Endings*. His most recent book is non-fiction history *Abraham Lincoln: Seldom Told Stories*. He is an active member of Mystery Writers of America and a lifetime member of Sisters in Crime with no hope of parole. He blogs on Fridays on the "Writers Who Kill" blog. His website is www.WarrenBull.com